Charles Busch's
The Tribute Artist

A Samuel French Acting Edition

SAMUELFRENCH.COM
SAMUELFRENCH-LONDON.CO.UK

MUSIC USE NOTE

Licensees are solely responsible for obtaining formal written permission from copyright owners to use copyrighted music in the performance of this play and are strongly cautioned to do so. If no such permission is obtained by the licensee, then the licensee must use only original music that the licensee owns and controls. Licensees are solely responsible and liable for all music clearances and shall indemnify the copyright owners of the play(s) and their licensing agent, Samuel French, against any costs, expenses, losses and liabilities arising from the use of music by licensees. Please contact the appropriate music licensing authority in your territory for the rights to any incidental music.

IMPORTANT BILLING AND CREDIT REQUIREMENTS

If you have obtained performance rights to this title, please refer to your licensing agreement for important billing and credit requirements.

THE TRIBUTE ARTIST was commissioned by Primary Stages and received its world premiere at Primary Stages (Casey Childs, Executive Producer; Andrew Leynse, Artistic Director; Elliot Fox, Managing Director) in association with Daryl Roth and Ted Snowdon at 59E59 Theaters in New York City on February 9, 2014. The performance was directed by Carl Andress, with sets by Anna Louizos, costumes by Gregory Gale, lighting by Kirk Bookman, sound by Jill BC Du Boff, music by Lewis Flynn, and wig design by Katherine Carr. The Production Stage Manager was Trisha Henson. The cast was as follows:

RITA . . . . .Julie Halston

ADRIANA. . . . . Cynthia Harris

JIMMY . . . . .Charles Busch

CHRISTINA. . . . . .Mary Bacon

RACHEL (OLIVER) . . . . Keira Keeley

RODNEY . . . . .Jonathan Walker

CHARACTERS

RITA
ADRIANA
JIMMY
CHRISTINA
RACHEL (OLIVER)
RODNEY

CASTING NOTE

The role of Jimmy requires an actor who can convincingly pass as a dignified, elegant older woman. It's not a broad campy impersonation. The story demands that the other characters believe that Jimmy is Adriana and it's important that the audience believe as well. Therefore, the actors playing Jimmy and Adriana must be generally the same height and weight. Christina and Rodney haven't seen Adriana in thirty years, so their memories of her can be somewhat vague, but there must be a realism in the new "Adriana" that they are meeting once again.

SETTING

The first floor of a four story townhouse in Greenwich Village

TIME

The Present

ACT ONE

Scene One

(The first floor of a four story townhouse in Greenwich Village. A front parlor with a staircase leading to the second floor. A pair of pocket doors separate this room from the entrance way. ADRIANA, an elegant older woman is seated. She speaks with a slight but indefinable European accent. RITA, a seen-it-all younger woman, is wearing a bright colored couture gown that doesn't suit her at all. A chic feather boa hangs around her neck. She pours herself another glass of wine.)

RITA. Can I take this dress? It's a great color for me. I'm a spring with autumn accents.

ADRIANA. Rita, my pet, that color could not be more wrong for you. And the cut. I designed that dress to be worn by a woman elegantly reed thin.

RITA. I have been often told that I have an aristocratic silhouette.

ADRIANA. By whom? No. You're of common clay; a quality highly valued in today's world. *(She shouts to **JIMMY** upstairs.)* What's taking so long? I want to see you in that gown! *(to **RITA**)* Such innate refinement and delicacy. With those magnificent bones the child can wear anything.

RITA. But, Adriana, he's a man. Anyway, Jimmy's upstairs. He can't hear you. I'd like to try it on next.

ADRIANA. I don't think so. That gown would wear *you.*

RITA. I may lack refinement but I am a very big personality. That's how I sell apartments.

ADRIANA. And not too many from what Jimmy tells me.

RITA. It's the economy.

ADRIANA. Is that so?

RITA. It's the economy.

ADRIANA. Didn't Jimmy tell me that some website listed you as the worst real estate agent in Manhattan?

RITA. That is not true. I got one and a half stars out of four. That was about average. Jimmy!

ADRIANA. One and a half out of four. Doesn't sound encouraging. When the small coterie of women I designed for began dying off, I left the business.

RITA. It didn't hurt having a rich husband. My last two girlfriends worked for Amtrack. They got decent retirement benefits, but not enough to reside like exiled royalty.

ADRIANA. Is that how you think I live? Well, I was fortunate to have the means to retreat within the walls of this townhouse.

RITA. I bet you entertained a lot in your glory days.

ADRIANA. Between my husband's work with the United Nations and my career, there were weeks where we had a dinner party nearly every night. Nehru once sat in that very chair. *(with condescension)* And now you.

RITA. Enough with the digs. Adriana, I don't know why you've never liked me. Believe it or not, most people find me captivating.

ADRIANA. I don't dislike you. I hardly know you.

RITA. Come on. Jimmy's been staying here for years. And I'm always around.

ADRIANA. Two years.

RITA. More like four years.

ADRIANA. Has it been that long? But he's only here, for what, two weeks at most? And then not for another six months. For that I should consider you a *bonne amie?*

RITA. No, but do you have to be so nasty?

ADRIANA. I think you're confusing nastiness with a European sense of irony.

RITA. But it's always at my expense. Sometimes my feelings can actually be hurt.

ADRIANA. I didn't realize you were such a delicate creature.

RITA. Well, I am.

ADRIANA. I can see that. I shall try and temper my astringent manner. It was never my intention to wound you.

(*She studies the way* **RITA** *has wrapped the boa around her neck.*)

RITA. Well, maybe now we can relate to each other on a more…. What's wrong?

ADRIANA. It's just fascinating how that boa looked expensive until you put it on.

(**JIMMY** *calls from upstairs.*)

JIMMY. (*offstage*) Are you ready?

RITA. We've been ready for an eternity.

JIMMY. Well, here I come!

(**JIMMY** *comes down the stairs dressed, wigged and made up exactly like* **ADRIANA.** *He imitates her voice exactly. Slim and elegant, he looks very realistically female.*)

JIMMY. (*as* **ADRIANA**) Well, Cherie, say something? Are you mute? (*referring to* **RITA**) Tell that bourgeois cow to put down that boa. Everything she touches looks positively Fourteenth Street.

RITA. That's perfect! He's totally you!

ADRIANA. That is not me. I worked very hard with a renowned speech coach to erase any trace of an accent.

JIMMY. (*as* **ADRIANA**) And, my dear, you were remarkably successful.

ADRIANA. I was.

JIMMY. (*as* **ADRIANA**) You were. Anyone with a brain would assume you were born in Tallahassee. (*He drops the accent.*) This is a great wig. When do you wear it?

ADRIANA. Silly question. When I don't feel like doing my own hair. Want it? It's yours.

JIMMY. Thanks, but it doesn't fit any of my impersonations, and I don't wear women's wigs in real life.

ADRIANA. Well, you never know, said the widow.

JIMMY. What does that mean?

ADRIANA. You never heard that phrase? The widow is open to whatever life has to offer. Erotic or otherwise. So take the wig. *(matter of factly)* You're a gorgeous drag queen.

JIMMY. Adriana, please don't call me a drag queen. You know I hate that.

RITA. Here we go.

ADRIANA. Words, words, words.

JIMMY. I'm a celebrity tribute artist.

ADRIANA. Yeah, yeah, yeah.

JIMMY. I recreate legendary female performers. I'm an illusionist. I don't do this for fun. I'm a professional entertainer.

RITA. How long do we get the pleasure of your company this time? When do you have to go back?

JIMMY. I'm not going back.

RITA. It never works when you hold out for more money. You always buckle.

JIMMY. I didn't buckle. *(to* **ADRIANA***)* Is this from the sixties?

RITA. So why aren't you going back?

JIMMY. What am I on trial? *Witness for the Prosecution?* I was let go. Terminated. The Vegas finger.

RITA. They fired you after all these years? I can't believe it.

ADRIANA. There is no loyalty in this world.

RITA. But you're lauded for your Marilyn and your Pearl Bailey. I can't believe it.

JIMMY. Wouldja please stop saying that? Believe it. There is no longer any place for Jimmy Nichols in the Flamingo Hotel's Boys Will Be Girls Revue. I should have seen the writing on the wall. Last year, both my Julie Andrews and Charo were cut. Finally, I was just left with Marilyn. She is my masterpiece but most of that Vegas crowd just thinks I'm doing Christina Aguilera. Everything's fallen apart since this new producer took over. He's a kid. He's forty years old.

RITA. The new producer – what's his name? Gary? Weren't you going with him?

JIMMY. Yeah.

RITA. And he still fired you?

JIMMY. Yeah.

RITA. You told me on the phone that the two of you were getting married.

ADRIANA. Married?

JIMMY. We went to the Fred Leighton store at the Bellagio and looked at rings. Little did I know he made the same promise to Jennifer Lopez. I mean the drag Jennifer Lopez, a skanky Mexican queen named Jorge. And it turns out Gary was also boffing the drag Katy Perry. I was totally blindsided. And it gets worse.

RITA. How does it get *worse?*

JIMMY. While I was onstage giving my final performance, Gary had the locks changed on the condo I was renting from him. I had to slip the handyman a hundred bucks to break the locks so I could get my things out.

ADRIANA. That's awful!

JIMMY. I still think, in his own way, Gary really loved me.

RITA. Oh, Jimmy, please.

JIMMY. Rita, you don't know Vegas. He had to make an executive decision. Audiences out there want impersonators who can do Rihanna or Beyonce. Liza and Cher are still in the show but, trust me, their necks will soon be on the chopping block. I'm finished. My expiration date is the same as the ladies I impersonate.

ADRIANA. That is a pity. From the video you showed me, you play women so convincingly.

RITA. Except for Jimmy, I find most drag misogynistic. *(unintentionally sounding like a braying, strident harridan)* Why must they all portray women as braying, strident harridans?

ADRIANA. You have a great empathy for women.

JIMMY. I was raised by my grandmother. I dunno.

ADRIANA. Did she want you to be a girl?

JIMMY. No. A gastroenterologist.

ADRIANA. Do you receive a form of sexual gratification from dressing in women's clothes? The soft fabrics? the close fitting garments?

JIMMY. No! This is just what I do best. Like juggling. You don't ask a juggler if he finds his balls sexually stimulating. Bad example.

RITA. He got into drag by accident and it's all because of me. Jimmy and I had a comedy improv act.

ADRIANA. *You* were on the stage?

RITA. Yes, Adriana. I was on the stage. When I met Jimmy I was doing stand-up.

ADRIANA. I can't see it. I've never found you remotely amusing.

RITA. I'll have you know I was nominated by the Manhattan Academy of Comedy Arts and Sciences as Outstanding Up and Coming Female Comic.

JIMMY. I was a makeup artist at the Shiseido counter at Macy's and I was going through a rough patch. I had just broken up with my boyfriend at the time. In retrospect I suppose I gave up on him too easily.

RITA. He burned all your clothes.

JIMMY. Yeah, well —

RITA. And then had *you* arrested for setting fire to the apartment.

JIMMY. Must you always focus on the negative? Anyway, Adriana, the point is I was sleeping on a friend's sofa who lived upstairs from a cabaret and sometimes I'd go downstairs and hang out at the bar and that's where I met *this* dame, holding forth over the cocktail onions.

RITA. And while we were enjoying our cocktails, we'd banter back and forth. Doing different character voices. We'd have the entire bar in stitches. Finally, the bartender suggested we do an act together. Fade out, fade in, we started doing Monday nights.

ADRIANA. And you were in drag?

JIMMY. I wasn't even playing female characters. I was always the guy in all of our sketches.

RITA. The thing is he just wasn't all that funny as the psychiatrist or the soft ball coach. I kept telling him the female celebrity impersonations he did for me afterwards privately were the gold.

JIMMY. So one night while we were doing our sketch about the line at the unemployment office, suddenly I became Mae West. *(as Mae West)* "Oh, how do I apply for an extension?"

RITA. It went over like gangbusters.

ADRIANA. I have no doubt.

JIMMY. We kept it in the act and then I added Katharine Hepburn. *(as Katharine Hepburn)* "Social security was taken out of my paycheck and by golly, I want those benefits!"

RITA. I'd be the woman behind the desk and I'd say "Miss Davis, I see here an opening for a food server at a health food restaurant."

JIMMY. *(as Bette Davis)* You bitch, I have far better things to do than stuff hummos in a pita. Pita, Pita, Pita!

ADRIANA. Oh, Bette Davis. She was once here for dinner.

RITA. Miss Davis, you are taking advantage of my good nature because I'm behind this desk.

JIMMY. *(as Bette Davis)* But you are behind the desk! You are! *(back to himself)* Bette Davis was here for dinner?

ADRIANA. I'll tell you about it later. Go on.

RITA. His impersonations became the act. At a certain point it became obvious that he didn't need me. And frankly, I'd had enough. I wanted to earn a living. I wanted credit cards. So I got my real estate license.

JIMMY. And then I got cast in a Vegas revue. I would never have dreamed I'd be there for a hundred years. And as a female impersonator yet. But I found that I could become these ladies. They're in me *(as Bette Davis)* and I just let 'em out.

ADRIANA. It's like Kabuki. No one ever coached you on how to be an American *Onnagata*?

JIMMY. I just knew how to walk in heels. But what do I do with this great gift that's completely unmarketable? I don't want to think about it now. *(as Vivien Leigh)* I'll think about it tomorrow. *(back to himself)* Or maybe the week after.

ADRIANA. Well, you had better make a plan soon. I don't know how much longer this house will be available.

JIMMY. What? Are you going away?

ADRIANA. I believe quite soon.

JIMMY. You feel strong enough to move? Where are you gonna live? Barcelona? Rome? Acapulco?

RITA. Jimmy, don't be dense. *(to ADRIANA)* Adriana, what makes you think the end is near?

ADRIANA. Just a feeling. A good feeling.

JIMMY. The end? Gosh, I don't know what to say.

ADRIANA. Say "Nice knowing you."

JIMMY. I don't see you very often but I always look forward to coming here. You've been very sweet to me in your sulfuric acid kind of way. Your florist, not even a close friend but your florist, told you his female impersonator buddy needed a room in New York and you took me in. You took me in. You charged me rent and raised it twice in four years but you took me in.

ADRIANA. You're the only one I ever let stay here.

JIMMY. I'll miss you.

ADRIANA. Oh, don't look at me like that, Jimmy. It's wonderful having no family or friends to shroud me with false sympathy.

JIMMY. Did you just find out?

ADRIANA. You love the melodrama. It was nothing like that. A year ago I told all my doctors to rot in hell. They wanted to keep me alive to fatten up their bank accounts. Forty-two pills they had me taking. I threw them into the garbage. The great physicians must all assume I'm long dead. And everyone else for that matter. You're the only one who ever visits. I haven't stepped out of this house in months. Thank God for the computer. I was a fool to resist it for so long.

JIMMY. You email people?

ADRIANA. Of course not. Anyone worth writing to is in their grave. I use it to pay my bills. I do all my banking on the computer. Everything. I have a notebook upstairs in my desk; an old notebook held together with scotch tape and Band-Aids, filled with numbers and passwords. I don't even have to bother making out a will. No one to leave anything to. Haven't had a lawyer in years. Shysters all of them.

RITA. You don't have a will? So who gets this house?

JIMMY. Rita!

RITA. I'm in real estate. I ask these questions.

ADRIANA. I have no idea. The bank? Or someone might turn up. They usually do. And when I'm cremated I want my ashes tossed into the toilet and I hope someone gives it a good strong flush and sends me down to China.

RITA. You're a hard hearted woman.

ADRIANA. I created a Faberge egg around my heart from early childhood. Only once was there a crack in that egg. Only once did I allow myself to feel.

JIMMY. Your husband?

ADRIANA. No, it was not my husband. Rodney Ash.

JIMMY. Rodney Ash. I love that name.

ADRIANA. I gave it to him.

JIMMY. Were you very young when you met?

ADRIANA. I was in my fifties, but looked great. He was almost young enough to be my grandson. That was something new for me. My husband was quite a bit older than I.

JIMMY. Was Rodney in fashion?

ADRIANA. Beauty such as his will always be in fashion. We were having a call for female models. And this wonderful looking young man walked in the door. When I told him that we had no need for a male model, that I only designed women's wear, he replied "Then I have no need for you." Such arrogance in a young man with a grey stain around his shirt collar. By evening, the shirt came off. Then everything came off. Rodney Ash possessed the most exquisite loins of any man I've ever known.

JIMMY. Whatja say?

RITA. Loins. She said loins.

ADRIANA. He had a small tattoo of a scorpion hidden underneath his scrotum. Should have been a warning. Do you know the mark of a true killer? He enjoyed being found out. He'd be caught stealing and he'd grin. Grin with the teeth I paid for. The last time I saw him was about a year after he left me. It was at a concert at Carnegie Hall. He was escorting a retired Bulgarian contralto. Our eyes met and in that one moment, he knew that I forgave him. My husband had long before forgiven *me.* I made it up to him. I entertained his colleagues. I took great care of his beloved townhouse. There was only one thing I denied him. I could not abide his dreadful family. His dreary sister and her daughter.

JIMMY. Where were they from?

ADRIANA. Where were they from? Chicago? Wyoming? The one time they came to visit I thought I would go mad. That ever so nice slob of a peasant woman. And her awful homely little girl. His niece, Christina. She kept staring at me, like a demon child in a science fiction.

I said to her, "What do you want from me? Go away, Changeling. Scat." I made my husband promise I would never have to endure his repugnant relations ever again. And he kept to his word. That was their one and only visit. Yet in my dreams I still see that pale little face with its pig-like eyes and snout and blubber lips.

Scene Two

(A few hours later. Three in the morning. **JIMMY***, still with the wig on, is asleep in one chair,* **RITA** *in the other chair.* **ADRIANA***, is lying on the sofa.* **JIMMY** *awakes.)*

JIMMY. What time is it? Rita. Rita. Wake up.

RITA. What's goin' on?

JIMMY. We both conked out. I'm going upstairs. You going home? You can spend the night.

RITA. What time is it?

JIMMY. Three thirty.

RITA. I feel like I've been in a coma. I've gotta get out of this dress.

JIMMY. Shhhhh. She's asleep. *(sees her eyes)* Oh, you're not. I'm sorry. I hope we didn't wake you.

RITA. I don't know what she's talking about. I look great in this color.

JIMMY. Adriana? Something's weird. Adriana?

RITA. Oh God. She's not – Is she?

JIMMY. Stone cold. She died in her sleep. We didn't even know. We didn't even know.

RITA. Wow. This makes three. This is more than a coincidence.

JIMMY. What coincidence?

RITA. She's the third person to die in a room I was in without my knowledge.

JIMMY. I wouldn't spread that around.

RITA. Each time I was out cold. Anyway, Adriana is the only one I actually knew.

JIMMY. I'm closing her eyes. *(He does that.)* I thought death was supposed to be ugly. Darling, you look marvelous.

RITA. You know, I almost feel like crying. I'm gonna say a little prayer. A Hail Mary.

JIMMY. So what do we do now? You're the expert. Call the police? 911?

RITA. I can't believe she didn't make any provisions for the sale of this house. A property like this in the West Village, even in this condition, can go for at least twelve million.

JIMMY. Who will get the twelve million?

RITA. It'll be absorbed into some city or federal bureaucracy. I know you liked her but that was a crummy thing to do. She could have left you a little cash. You were very kind to her.

JIMMY. I saw her for two weeks twice a year. She didn't owe me anything. Not really.

RITA. If I could get my hands on this house, I could find a buyer like this. *(snaps her fingers)*

JIMMY. You could do that, huh?

RITA. Like this. *(She snaps her fingers again.)* If I sold this house , we'd split the entire thing fifty fifty. Six million for each of us.

JIMMY. How can we sell a house that's not ours?

RITA. What if Adriana lived a little bit longer, at least long enough to sell the house?

JIMMY. I do a great impersonation of her.

RITA. And it's not even necessary. No one's seen her for months. She has no relatives, no friends. She has no doctors.

JIMMY. No lawyer.

RITA. What about the cleaning girl?

JIMMY. She's doing a lousy job. I used to clean apartments. She's terrible. One phone call. Goodbye.

RITA. So *she's* out of the way. But in every movie where someone is posing as the heir to a fortune or their own twin sister, there's always some forgotten detail that trips them up.

JIMMY. You're right. You're right. And if it doesn't work in the movies, why would it work in real life? It was a stupid idea. Crime never pays.

RITA. But is it really a crime?

JIMMY. Impersonating a dead person? Yes. Forget it, honey. This house doesn't belong to us.

RITA. But who does it belong to? No one.

JIMMY. Forget it. So can I crash on your sofa until I figure out what I'm going to do?

RITA. Sure.

JIMMY. What *am* I going to do? Get into a Broadway show? I don't have an agent. I don't even belong to Actor's Equity. I don't exist. Even if I leave the business, what sort of job could I hope to find at my age? I have no savings. I'll never be able to get my name on a lease. Old and indigent. That's my fate. It's not an attractive one.

RITA. The way things are going, I'll be in the same boat. Destitute, homeless, swigging rubbing alcohol, Listerine, anything I can lay my hands on.

JIMMY. What did she say? She has a notebook with all her passwords in it? *(laughs bitterly)* She's handing us our future on a silver platter. But we don't dare touch it.

RITA. If only we had the guts to follow through on something like this, but we don't. We're small people, Jimmy.

JIMMY. If we only had the guts. If we only had the guts. We have the guts, Rita. We have the guts. Desperation gives you the guts. Why shouldn't we survive? Why shouldn't we know happiness? Why shouldn't we know luxury? We're not bad people. We've made bad choices. We've been stooges! We've been patsies! The fall guy. We deserve to live out our lives with dignity and respect and a healthy stock portfolio.

RITA. You're making me feel light headed and a little nauseous.

JIMMY. That's how you feel, Rita, that's how you feel when you're a winner. We're not losers any more. We've won! We've won!

RITA. Oh my God. Are we really going to do this?

JIMMY. We gotta think clearly. This is precisely the moment when the fatal error is made.

RITA. I'm sober as a judge and totally with you.

JIMMY. And, you're gonna have to remain sober if we're gonna pull this off.

RITA. Not even a glass of Chardonnay at Happy Hour. Just a Sprite with lime and bitters.

JIMMY. The first step is what do we do with Adriana? What do we do with the body?

RITA. Well, I guess the easiest solution is to cut her into pieces and disintegrate the remains with lye.

JIMMY. *(aghast)* That's the easiest? I couldn't cut her up. She was my friend and I've made a mess out of a rotisserie chicken.

RITA. I'm just saying –

JIMMY. I'm not sure this plan is bringing out the best in you.

RITA. Okay. Dismemberment is not an option.

JIMMY. We can't ever be in the position where we could possibly be accused of murder. The lady died of natural causes. That's our safety net. We need to call 911 and have them take her away, but they've got to think she's somebody else. We need to pin a fake ID on her. How many times in Vegas has someone offered to make me a fake ID? I never anticipate. That's my tragedy.

RITA. I have a fake ID.

JIMMY. You have a fake ID?

RITA. Yeah.

(She takes her wallet out of her bag and searches through her cards.)

JIMMY. She has a fake ID. I can't believe this.

RITA. Here. Look. Phyllis Robbins. New York State driver's license.

JIMMY. What are you doing with that? And who's Phyllis Robbins?

RITA. *I'm* Phyllis Robbins. Remember Antoinetta? Her cousin Ray makes these for a living. A Christmas present. A veritable work of art. But will it get past the police?

JIMMY. The lighting is hideous. Doesn't even look like you. And why is your hair slicked back like LBJ?

RITA. It was taken at a women's fest in P'town. Enough with the picture. With her hair pulled back, there's no reason she couldn't be Phyllis Robbins.

JIMMY. Last night, when I told Adriana this wig didn't fit any of my impersonations, she said "You never know, said the widow." She was planting the idea in my head. She wanted me to do this.

RITA. I think she did. I can hear her laughing. I never liked her laugh.

JIMMY. How long do you anticipate this whole thing should take? Selling the house.

RITA. With this location? Give me two months. One month if we take the first bid.

JIMMY. And when the dust settles and the checks clear, we report Adriana's death from somewhere in Europe. I do believe the south of France is quite lovely this time of year.

RITA. The plan is fool proof.

JIMMY. It's fool proof because it's simple. Can we just say it? We're geniuses.

RITA. We're geniuses, Jimmy.

JIMMY. Thank you, Adriana. Merci, cherie. Let's call 911.

Scene Three

*(Several weeks later. Afternoon. **ADRIANA**'s niece,
CHRISTINA, and her fifteen year old grand-niece,
RACHEL, are seated on the settee. **CHRISTINA**, once "the
homely little girl" is now an attractive woman. Well,
she'd be very attractive if hard knocks hadn't given her a
perpetually troubled and suspicious expression. **RACHEL**
is transgendered. She looks and acts convincingly like a
boy and wants to be called "**OLIVER**".)*

CHRISTINA. There's something sort of wonderful when
your worst nightmare becomes a reality.

RACHEL. Mom, please don't do this to yourself.

CHRISTINA. No, I'm trying to look on the bright side.
My life has always been a rocky road of failure and
frustration, except for you, Sweetie. Of course, my
Aunt would try and steal my inheritance. It's perfect.

RACHEL. She's gonna be down any minute. She'll hear
us. Mom, she's lived in this house for over forty
years. She's probably convinced herself that she owns
it. Anyway, I love Aunt Adriana with all my heart.

CHRISTINA. You met her seven minutes ago. You've got to
toughen up. We live in a very harsh modern world.

RACHEL. You don't have to tell me that.

CHRISTINA. There are people everywhere who will stop at
nothing to dupe us out of what is legally ours.

RACHEL. Mom, I hate when you get like this.

CHRISTINA. Well, the vengeful creature that you see
before you is what the world has made of me.
I am the product of my parent's negligence, my
teacher's carelessness, your father's abandonment,
my employer's exploitation and um – I'm sure there
others I'm forgetting.

RACHEL. I'm grateful for that.

CHRISTINA. Sweetie, do you know why I have for years subscribed to the New York Times even though we live in Wisconsin and I can barely afford it?

RACHEL. I dunno. To keep up with the world?

CHRISTINA. So I could comb through the obituaries every day with the desperate hope that Aunt Adriana's name would appear and I could finally claim what is rightfully ours.

RACHEL. That is so creepy.

CHRISTINA. It is creepy. I'm creepy, but what's more creepy is that my Aunt would think she could perpetrate this fraud without my knowing. Like I'm such a moron.

RACHEL. You're projecting what's in her head. It's a complicated situation.

CHRISTINA. No. It's very simple. Uncle Lou willed this house to his only surviving blood relative; me. Me. But in a ridiculous clause, his evil widow could live here until her death.

RACHEL. Stop. Please. It's like you're stuck on "repeat."

CHRISTINA. I'll keep going until I get one hundred per cent sympathy from you. Aunt Adriana cannot under any circumstances sell this house. And that's precisely what she's trying to do. She's stealing my personal property. She's stealing your future! She is stealing our only hope for survival!

RACHEL. You're turning it into some kind of personal attack. This is so you. Dr. Beckerman says you're trapped in a web of misplaced emotion.

CHRISTINA. I'm grateful that you've found Dr. Beckerman and that he's been such a supporter of yours, but he's an asshole.

RACHEL. He's not an asshole. He's a cognitive therapist. He's helped me see that your misguided choices have severely impacted my life.

CHRISTINA. *(starts to cry)* Oh God.

RACHEL. Mom, stop it. I'm not blaming you. You acted out of ignorance.

CHRISTINA. I wanted to give my little girl pretty things. I thought even tomboys like to dress up occasionally.

RACHEL. But I'm not a tomboy. I'm a transman. That's just the way it is.

CHRISTINA. What can I say? I'm an ignorant hick. I wanted to believe you were going through a phase.

RACHEL. You wanted to believe. Dr. Beckerman says that's your fatal flaw.

CHRISTINA. *(vulnerably)* He says I have a fatal flaw?

RACHEL. I'm paraphrasing. He said you get fantasies about people and refuse to see them as they are.

CHRISTINA. You've got to admit, you've thrown a lot at me in the past couple years.

RACHEL. And I'm gonna continue to do that as I become more comfortable with myself. I'm not ruling out a touch of androgyny. I just might surprise you one day by wearing a skirt.

CHRISTINA. Really?

RACHEL. More like a kilt. There you go with this kind of pathetic hope. How long did it take for you to finally see that Daddy wasn't in love with you and hated me?

CHRISTINA. He doesn't hate you.

RACHEL. He thinks I'm a freak and you're a neurotic mess and he doesn't want anything to do with us.

CHRISTINA. I'm not the type who gives up.

RACHEL. With you that's not a good trait. Dr. Beckerman says you confuse tenacity with wishful thinking. He says this gets in the way of your being a friend to yourself.

CHRISTINA. All right. Dr. Beckerman isn't an asshole. *I'm* the asshole. *I'm* the asshole.

(**JIMMY** *comes down the stairs dressed as* **ADRIANA**, *holding a delicate necklace.*)

JIMMY. Here it is, Cherie. I found it. It was upstairs in my sewing room.

CHRISTINA. What is this?

JIMMY. The garnet necklace you loved so much.

CHRISTINA. I don't remember this.

JIMMY. The first night of your visit to New York when you were a little girl, we went through all my jewelry. And this garnet necklace was your favorite.

CHRISTINA. That absolutely did not happen.

JIMMY. And yet I remember it as if it were yesterday.

RACHEL. Mom, maybe you've blocked out that one happy memory. *(to* **ADRIANA***)* She does this.

CHRISTINA. You don't understand. I have total recall of every moment of that visit. Every minute of every day.

JIMMY. Did we have great fun?

CHRISTINA. It was a disaster. You were unforgivably cruel to a vulnerable ten year old girl, who came here to worship her fabulous Aunt.

JIMMY. Cruel to a child? *C'est impossible.*

CHRISTINA. You would have nothing to do with me. When Uncle Lou suggested you take me to the Central Park Zoo, you said I should *be* in the zoo. That night I overheard you telling Uncle Lou that I had pig eyes and blubber lips.

JIMMY. Pigs are treasured in France. *Les cochons.* But do take the necklace. I want you to have it.

CHRISTINA. You're not buying me off with a crappy garnet necklace.

RACHEL. Mom –

JIMMY. Oliver, darling, let her speak.

CHRISTINA. You can't fool me with your gracious Lady Bountiful act.

JIMMY. She accuses me of putting on an act.

CHRISTINA. I refuse to believe that you aren't perfectly aware that this house is not yours to sell.

(**RITA** *fairly bursts through the front door, carrying a box of donuts.*)

RITA. I've got donuts! Vanilla frosted, chocolate and glazed! Hello, you must be Christina and you must be Oliver. I'm Rita Loffredo. I got here as soon as I could.

CHRISTINA. Rita Loffredo. The broker who tried to sell the house? I have nothing to say to you.

RACHEL. My mother's been under a lot of stress.

RITA. Christina, your Aunt is of an age where she needs to simplify her lifestyle.

CHRISTINA. I'm not interested.

RITA. She is finding it increasingly difficult going up and down those stairs with her hips, her knees and a prolapsed uterus.

JIMMY. I feel it falling right now.

RITA. I found a buyer willing to pay twelve million dollars for this property. It was a *fait accompli.*

CHRISTINA. Yeah, until his lawyer did a routine search and discovered that the house wasn't hers to sell.

RITA. It was a *fait accompli.* Twelve million dollars, Christina, is more than enough to amply provide both you and your Aunt with income for life.

RACHEL. Six million sounds great.

CHRISTINA. Uncle Lou willed this house to me so I could sell it and have *all* the income because he loved me. Yes. He loved me. And even though because of *her* I was forbidden to ever enter this house after the age of ten, he used to fly to Milwaukee once a year and treated me like a Princess.

RITA. It's not unheard of for you and your Aunt to make an agreement to merge your interests and sell the property.

CHRISTINA. Why should I share the money with her? She never expressed any interest in me.

JIMMY. Is it too late to begin now?

CHRISTINA. Oh, come off it.

JIMMY. *(sounding very Joan Crawford)* Christina, darling, I have made grave mistakes in my life. If I've hurt you, I would gladly cut off my hand.

RITA. Adriana, you're not yourself.

JIMMY. I'm so upset. I don't know who I am.

CHRISTINA. I don't know who you are either. It's been so many years. You're almost unrecognizable to me.

RITA. Age can make one almost unrecognizable. People used to tell me that I was the spitting image of Daryl Hannah. Look at me now. I've developed an almost masculine look.

JIMMY. That's what happens when one gets older. The genders become blurred. I tell you, without my wig and makeup, I...look like a man.

RITA. Observe closely and you'll see a moustache. She's dispensed with all depilatory treatments.

RACHEL. *(pointedly for her mother's benefit)* I could grow a moustache if I went on hormones.

CHRISTINA. This conversation should be between our lawyers, as soon as I find one...pro bono.

JIMMY. My darling, I don't want to beg for compassion but time is of the essence.

RACHEL. Oh, Aunt Adriana.

JIMMY. That's one of the reasons I wish to return to Europe.

CHRISTINA. We have to go.

JIMMY. In Europe perhaps I can be reunited with my great love; Rodney Ash. *(sounding a lot like Greta Garbo)* Rodney was the only one who broke through that Faberge egg I had created around my heart.

RACHEL. When was the last time you saw him?

JIMMY. More than twenty years ago.

RACHEL. Do you know how to find him?

RITA. There's always the Internet. She's surprisingly facile with the computer.

RACHEL. Maybe he's right here in New York. Mom, isn't there a compromise? Can't we split the money with her?

CHRISTINA. Will you *never* be on my side?

RITA. You have your health. That's more than your Aunt can say.

CHRISTINA. Oh yes, I'm very lucky. That ought to be my name. "Lucky." Let me show you the fruits of my good fortune. *(She digs into her bag, finds the folded letter and opens it.)*

RACHEL. Mother, don't.

CHRISTINA. Allow me to read you my annual Christmas letter.

RACHEL. Mother, please.

CHRISTINA. "To all who read this; It's been quite a year. I recovered from the torn tendon in my ankle and no longer have to wear the orthopedic boot. However, two days later, in frustration I kicked our broken refrigerator door and fractured my big toe. I am unable to heal myself physically, emotionally or spiritually. My son Oliver is as always the one bright shining light in my otherwise bleak existence. If you're wondering why I never mentioned I had a son, it's because until four months ago, he was my daughter who you have known as Rachel. Oliver has begun his transition to becoming the male he has always known himself to be. He has been my rock in these awful months since I was laid off at the beauty salon. We've had to severely cut expenses. First to go were our premium cable channels. HBO and Showtime. Then the DVR, then basic cable. While watching the Golden Globe Awards, the TV itself, a twelve-year-old Panasonic, blew out and I can't afford to replace it. Among other cost saving measures, I've stopped using any moisturizers and now my skin is feeling uncomfortably dry and leathery. My lips are forever chapped. In September, my best friend from work, Melanie, died after a long illness. She was the sibling I never had. One day while she was dozing, I came across her journal. Perhaps it was wrong of me to read it but in one of her last entries, she wrote "My dying wish is that Christina would *not* pay me any more visits. She's so fucking depressing, terminal cancer is more fun." That's all the news for now. Happy holidays and may your next year be better than mine."

RACHEL. I can't believe you sent that out. You are so ridiculously fill of self-pity.

JIMMY. You must not speak to your mother that way.

RITA. Adriana, this is between them.

RACHEL. Her negativity is destroying our lives.

CHRISTINA. I'm trying to *save* our lives.

RACHEL. Don't try so hard. I mean, here we are in New York City. My first time here. Your first visit since you were ten, and there hasn't been one split second that you haven't been in a total rage.

CHRISTINA. Yes, I'm in a continual rage against this woman who is determined to cheat us.

JIMMY. But should that stop you from taking in a Broadway show?

CHRISTINA. This whole trip is on a credit card I can't hope to pay off.

RACHEL. Well, I'm not going back with you. I'm spending the summer in New York.

RITA. How are you planning on doing that?

RACHEL. I'm going to stay here.

JIMMY. What?

RACHEL. Aunt Adriana, you've got all these empty rooms upstairs. Can't I stay here, please?

CHRISTINA. Absolutely not. You're flying back with me Sunday night.

JIMMY. My darling, there's nothing I should like more than for you to spend the summer with me, but I could not allow you to disobey your mother.

RACHEL. Please, Aunt Adriana, please let me stay here. I can take care of you. I take care of my mother and she's half your age.

RITA. This is marvelous that you've finally met your Great Aunt Adriana and when you go back to Milwaukee you'll stay in touch. And maybe on Christmas vacation –

RACHEL. I'm not going back.

CHRISTINA. She hates where we live.

RACHEL. No. Everybody where we live hates *me.* I have no friends. I only have enemies who want to physically hurt me. You have no idea what it's like. You think you do but you don't.

CHRISTINA. All right. You can stay in New York. You can stay here in this house. But then so am I.

JIMMY. What just happened?

CHRISTINA. You've got plenty of rooms here. I owe it to myself. I'm owed an adventure.

RITA. How long are you planning on staying?

CHRISTINA. The rest of the summer.

RACHEL. Wow. You're actually going to do something good for yourself. I can't believe it.

JIMMY. But don't you have to return to Milwaukee? Surely you have a job.

CHRISTINA. Weren't you listening? I was laid off. There's nothing for me there. I can collect my unemployment benefits online.

JIMMY. But considering how much you despise me, would you not prefer to stay somewhere else?

CHRISTINA. I can't afford anywhere else. And *considering* how you've been plotting to deny me my inheritance, putting us up is the very least you could do. The *very* least.

JIMMY. Rita, say something.

CHRISTINA. Let's check out of the motor lodge right now and bring our stuff back here.

RITA. Whoa. Whoa. Whoa. Hold on just a minute. This isn't sleep away camp. Even if this house isn't technically Adriana's to sell, it's still her home until she passes on.

CHRISTINA. Ms. Loffredo, if you wish to begin any sort of negotiation with me regarding the sale of this property, you would do well not to antagonize me. Come on, Sweetie. If we hurry, we can check out before noon.

RACHEL. This is so – Oh God! I love you, Aunt Adriana, till the end of time.

(*She gives* **JIMMY** *a big hug and they exit.*)

RITA. Take off that drag and let's beat it! We've got less than an hour before they get back.

JIMMY. Couldn't you see that Christina was beginning to soften up?

RITA. Forget about *her*. The kid's gonna blow your cover.

JIMMY. Why? He's crazy about me.

RITA. He's transgender.

JIMMY. What are you talking about?

RITA. He's transgender. He used to be a girl.

JIMMY. Where'd you get that?

RITA. Weren't you listening to the letter? Christina spelled it all out.

JIMMY. I couldn't get past her giving up HBO.

RITA. As usual, you hear only what you want to hear. Oliver is a transgendered kid and he's going to see right through you.

JIMMY. For six million dollars I can stay in costume. Christina thinks she remembers her Aunt but it's been decades. I'll be whoever they want me to be.

RITA. Don't be too creative. More than a couple of times, I noticed Aunt Adriana slipping into Joan Crawford and Garbo.

JIMMY. That's why I need you around to keep me on track. There are scads of rooms upstairs. The Madame DuBarry room. The Romanov bedroom. The Chinese whorehouse. Take your pick.

RITA. You want me to move in?

JIMMY. It'll be a hoot. Hey, look on the bright side, Christina is exactly your type.

RITA. My type?

JIMMY. Girly but tough and smart with no self-esteem. It's like you wrote a letter to Santa.

RITA. She's attractive but I don't get the slightest gay vibe from her.

JIMMY. You never know said the widow. You'd better get your stuff over here before they get back.

RITA. I still don't see how are you gonna make her turn around and split the money with us?

JIMMY. *(sweetly)* I've got to be kind, affectionate and caring and get the cunt to love me.

Scene Four

(Two weeks have passed. **RACHEL** *enters with* **ADRIANA**'s *old love,* **RODNEY ASH**. *Twenty-five years later, one can still see the beautiful young man he was, but this new seedy* **RODNEY** *is decidedly lived in. He holds an 8 x 10 manila envelope.)*

RODNEY. Ohh, that chair. The first time I was here I sat down and broke it. I was trying to act so cool and ended up with my big butt bouncing on the floor. Look. You can see where it was repaired.

RACHEL. I didn't picture you being a klutz.

RODNEY. *(picks up a cigarette box)* The marble cigarette box. Someone important gave it to her. *(searching)* Martha Graham? Graham Greene? Graham cracker? That's it. The head of Nabisco.

RACHEL. The corner is broken.

RODNEY. She threw it at me. I'd never seen a cigarette box before. I'd never seen an oriental rug. I was brought up on strictly wall to wall shag. And what we didn't walk on, we wore.

RACHEL. Does being back in this house bring back a lot of memories? I mean of you and Aunt Adriana?

RODNEY. The most beautiful days of my life. What a fool I was to have ended them so soon.

RACHEL. You were really young.

RODNEY. I was a son of a bitch prick bastard. Take a lesson from me, kid. If you're ever fortunate enough to meet a person of great wisdom, an oracle, don't take their gifts lightly.

RACHEL. I never get tired of hearing her stories.

RODNEY. I'm so jealous. I could wring your neck like a turkey for having the honor of listening to her.

RACHEL. Well, now you're back. I mean, like, three cheers for facebook.

RODNEY. Thank you for requesting to be my friend. No one's wanted to befriend me for a very long time.

RACHEL. Aunt Adriana spoke so beautifully about you.

RODNEY. She has? What'd she say?

RACHEL. Let me think. She said –

RODNEY. *(casually)* Did she tell you about the time I went down on her at the Frick?

RACHEL. *(uncomfortable)* No. But she talks about you a lot.

RODNEY. What did she say? I want specifics.

RACHEL. Lots of stuff. Don't put me on the spot.

RODNEY. I guess I'm finding the whole situation kind of unnerving.

RACHEL. When I saw that you lived in New York, I had to contact you.

RODNEY. And she's really forgiven me?

RACHEL. That's what she says.

RODNEY. When it was good, it was so good. She never told you about the time she went down on me at the Met?

RACHEL. No. She's my Great-Aunt.

RODNEY. *(shrugs)* My mother told *me* everything. In some ways you remind me of myself. When I was your age, I was a pretty boy like you. I'd go into a store and be mistaken for a girl. I used it. I can tell you're a brain. I bet you love school. Can't wait to get there in the morning. I hated every day of it.

RACHEL. I'm terrible at school. I might even be left back.

RODNEY. You're a rotten kid?

RACHEL. No. Just invisible.

(**CHRISTINA** *comes downstairs.*)

CHRISTINA. Hello. Is there something I can do for you?

RACHEL. This is Rodney Ash.

CHRISTINA. I'm Oliver's Mom. Do I know you?

RACHEL. Aunt Adriana's friend. The one she talks about.

CHRISTINA. The one she talks about?

RACHEL. Rodney Ash.

CHRISTINA. The guy she hasn't seen in decades?

RODNEY. It's been a long time.

RACHEL. I found him on facebook and amazingly he lives in New York.

CHRISTINA. Does Aunt Adriana know about this?

RACHEL. No. It's a surprise.

CHRISTINA. Rachel – Oliver, you can't do that to people.

RODNEY. Rachel Oliver? Maybe I should leave.

RACHEL. Don't.

CHRISTINA. I can't believe you did this. What were you thinking of? Life is harrowing enough without you making it more harrowing.

RACHEL. Mom, I'm sorry, I didn't mean to –

CHRISTINA. Your heart was in the right place. But you just don't know how people are going to react to a sudden surprise. You remember what happened to Melanie's Cousin Essie? *(to* **RODNEY***)* Some well-intentioned person reunited her with a long lost boyfriend who years before buried her up to her neck at Saugatuck Beach, dumped the three bean salad on her head and left her there. Ha. Ha. Ha. Practical joke. Seeing him again made her break out in Shingles. Or was it Bell's Palsy? Either way it was devastating.

RACHEL. Mom –

CHRISTINA. Don't take this personally but we don't know anything about you. Maybe you're the nicest guy in the world and my Aunt will be thrilled to see you. I don't know. I mean, you're obviously a good looking guy. Very striking. Personable. I mean, I'm your average, run of the mill kind of level-headed person, but if this happened to me, I'd be apoplectic.

RODNEY. I understand. I shouldn't have come here.

CHRISTINA. Thank you. You have an open honest face. You seem totally sincere. But Oliver was wrong to have established contact without her approval.

RACHEL. But she desperately wants to see you. For some reason, Aunt Adriana thought you were living in Italy. She was actually going to go over there to look for you.

RODNEY. Italy? How could she have known that I lived for six months in Milano? The woman's psychic. Did she tell you that while I was there a witch, a *strega*, put a hex on me? While I was asleep, she swiped some of my pubic hair.

CHRISTINA. Excuse me.

RODNEY. She must be very lonely living here all by herself.

RACHEL. She has a friend living with her. Rita. Do you remember her?

RODNEY. Rita?

CHRISTINA. Mannish, strident.

RODNEY. Was she in fashion?

CHRISTINA. No. Real estate. They went out for a walk. Probably plotting their next move.

RODNEY. What?

CHRISTINA. Never mind. I really think you should go before they get back.

RACHEL. I'll text you as soon as we break it to her.

RODNEY. Please don't forget. This means so much to me. My life.

(*The front door opens and it's* **RITA** *and* **JIMMY**. **JIMMY** *is garbed as* **ADRIANA**, *wearing slacks and draped in an elegant light shawl.*)

JIMMY. Hello, darling!

RODNEY. Adriana?

JIMMY. I beg your pardon.

RODNEY. You don't recognize me?

JIMMY. I'm afraid I don't. Should I?

RACHEL. Aunt Adriana, it's Rodney.

JIMMY. Rodney?

RACHEL. Rodney. Rodney Ash.

*(**JIMMY** topples over. **RACHEL** catches him.)*

CHRISTINA. Aunt Adriana, are you all right?

JIMMY. Rodney. How is it poss – Rodney?

RODNEY. Um Oliver found me on facebook. He gave me hope that you would consent to see me.

RITA. Well, isn't this something? This is really something.

JIMMY. *(discombobulated)* Forgive me, this is – *(He blanks on **RITA**'s name.)* I'm sorry. What's your name, dear?

RITA. Rita. Rita Loffredo. She's not always this bad.

CHRISTINA. She's disoriented. Aunt Adriana, who is the President of the United States?

JIMMY. Christina, cool it. Rodney, where have you been living?

RODNEY. Just a few subway stops away. You knew I had been in Italy. You're a sorceress.

RACHEL. It's like you have ESP.

RITA. I don't know how she comes up with these things.

JIMMY. I had a vision. There you were outside the Vatican, eating a Cannoli.

RODNEY. I can never forget the afternoons we spent in that dining room, side by side at the long oak table, pouring over art books. My education. You gave me Raphael, Botticelli and Tintoretto.

JIMMY. Ah yes, Tintoretto. *(at a loss)* So much talent. Alas, my memory is now but a blur of faces, pages of a calendar and the sound of trains passing through the night.

RODNEY. I brought some old photos of me to jog your memory. Nudes.

JIMMY. Let me see.

RODNEY. Why don't we wait till we're alone?

CHRISTINA. You can leave them with us. We'll be very careful with them.

JIMMY. Christina. *(to **RODNEY**)* I can never forget the first time you appeared in my studio.

RODNEY. Just me and a collection of the most beautiful girls in the world.

RITA. I remember this story. It's a good one.

JIMMY. And when I told you we had no need for a male model, you replied "Then I have no need for you."

RODNEY. Such arrogance. And yet you stopped me from leaving.

CHRISTINA. I guess you really do know each other. Forgive me for being so rude.

JIMMY. Please forgive *me* for not recognizing you immediately. How could I have forgotten those eyes? And that impossibly sensual mouth.

RODNEY. The mouth has changed. Too many cigarettes.

JIMMY. The mouth is the same. Is the kiss the same?

RITA. Perhaps we should all have a cup of tea.

CHRISTINA. Absolutely. Rodney, herbal or Liptons?

RACHEL. I think you should stay for dinner.

RODNEY. Let me hold you, dear Adriana.

RITA. Be very gentle with her. Her bones are as brittle as Saltines.

JIMMY. Yes, kiss me gently, like a dutiful son.

> (**RODNEY** *kisses "her" gently and pulls away.* **JIMMY** *takes hold of the sides of* **RODNEY***'s head and devouringly kisses him.*)

Scene Five

(Later that afternoon. **JIMMY** *and* **RODNEY** *are seated on the sofa looking at the photographs* **RODNEY** *brought with him.)*

RODNEY. You were standing right beside the camera when that picture was taken.

JIMMY. I was always surprised you didn't get more work from these test shots.

RODNEY. I wasn't really a model.

JIMMY. But so beautiful. My darling. So beautiful.

RODNEY. I was a pretty boy. Remember that time Lou was out of town and you dressed me up in drag?

JIMMY. Vaguely. Remind me again.

RODNEY. You put your Verdura diamond clips on my ears and then you got out your cosmetics and made me up; lipstick, false eye lashes, the works.

JIMMY. Yes, it's coming back. Tell me more.

RODNEY. You ordered me to take off all my clothes and you draped my naked body with ropes of pearls and about a dozen gold chains. And your cabochon emerald bracelets. Where are they now?

JIMMY. Sold years ago. But I have boxes and boxes of costume jewelry. I might demand a second performance.

RODNEY. I'm not a pretty boy anymore.

JIMMY. *(as Mae West)* You'll do.

*(***RODNEY*** *takes out another eight by ten.)*

RODNEY. Remember this one? I was in great shape then.

JIMMY. Look at that ass.

RODNEY. That's some ass. I shouldn't have stopped working out. The bigger mistake was leaving you.

JIMMY. You outgrew me.

RODNEY. Not true. I just outgrew my pants.

JIMMY. What does it matter? My place was with my husband. I've never regretted it.

RODNEY. I'm choking with regret. I was a horrible young man.

JIMMY. You hurt me. And yet, don't you remember years later, when I saw you again at Carnegie Hall? You were escorting some hairy arm-pitted Bulgarian Mezzo.

RODNEY. You remember that?

JIMMY. Our eyes met and I hoped that you saw that I'd forgiven you.

RODNEY. I wanted to believe that. Your memory is better than you think.

JIMMY. I remember your scorpion tattoo in that most provocative of secret places.

RODNEY. You're making me blush. Can we be serious for a moment?

JIMMY. *(removing the shawl)* Oh Rodney, I'm too old to be serious.

RODNEY. I've only been half alive since I left you.

JIMMY. You always had a flair for melodrama. Did you pursue acting?

RODNEY. I pursued actresses. I was convinced that the only way to make it in show business was by giving a good fuck. That qualified me to actually produce a film in Romania; a thriller starring the 1993 Miss Guatemala. The plot involved the trafficking of human body parts on the black market. Well, it turned out that the screenwriter wasn't working strictly from imagination. When it became clear that I hadn't raised all the money to finish the film, the writer and director had me kidnapped and tortured in a basement in a suburb of Bucharest. To be succinct and without a hint of melodrama, they stripped me naked and held my testicles in a vise.

JIMMY. Tell me everything.

RODNEY. They threatened me with castration unless I took on a little job for them.

JIMMY. What sort of job?

RODNEY. An acting job of sorts. I was required to impersonate a recently deceased American hospital employee in charge of the cadaver donating program. My task was to divert donated cadavers and process them so their body parts could be sold commercially. I wasn't dealing with major organs, no hearts for me, but you'd be amazed at the market value of spines, ears and cartilage. Pharmaceutical companies pay top dollar for finger nails.

JIMMY. We do what we must.

RODNEY. So many times I'd be working alone in that basement and I'd think about what I did to you. I got what I deserved. Over the course of the year I developed a tremor in my hands that made me not the ideal candidate for surgical precision, so eventually I was tossed out like one of my used up corpses. I returned to the U.S. and found a lady who could help me with my shaking. A most demanding mistress. I don't know why I'm trying to be so goddam clever. Heroin. I got hooked on smack. One fine spring morning I was found comatose and naked at the last stop of the Eighth Avenue subway. They locked me up in a charity rehab and I nearly died going cold turkey but I've stayed clean. I've also cleaned my share of public toilets. I'm not good for much else. I need rest, Adriana. I need for you to say it's all right.

JIMMY. My darling Rodney.

RODNEY. *(placing his head in* **JIMMY**'s *lap)* Take me back.

JIMMY. I'm not what I was.

(**RODNEY** *sniffs* **JIMMY**'s *wrist.*)

RODNEY. I remember that perfume. Your own special scent.

(**RODNEY** *moves* **JIMMY**'s *hand towards his crotch.* **JIMMY** *pulls himself away.*)

JIMMY. I'm not sure my heart can stand this.

(**RODNEY** *get up, throws off his coat and approaches* **JIMMY** *with animalistic passion.*)

JIMMY. Oh, Rodney.

(**RODNEY** *pushes* **JIMMY** *down on the sofa and runs his hands down* **JIMMY**'s *body.*)

RODNEY. This doesn't feel like the body of an old woman.

JIMMY. Until recently I did Pilates.

(**RODNEY** *moves his hands towards* **JIMMY**'s *crotch.*)

RODNEY. Remember the time we were dining at Le Cirque and I slid under the table?

JIMMY. Naughty boy, you shouldn't have done that and we shouldn't be doing this.

RODNEY. I never do what I'm told.

JIMMY. Please, stop. Someone might come in.

RODNEY. That never stopped us before.

(**RODNEY** *touches* **JIMMY**'s *groin and feels something decidedly male.*)

RODNEY. What is this?

JIMMY. Nothing important.

RODNEY. Oh my God! Oh my God!!

JIMMY. I've always been this way. You just never knew it.

RODNEY. Adriana didn't have a cock! Who are you? What have you done with Adriana?

JIMMY. She's dead.

RODNEY. You killed her! You freak! You killed her?

JIMMY. I didn't kill her. I swear I didn't.

RODNEY. How did you know about the tattoo under my balls?

JIMMY. Adriana told me. We were friends.

RODNEY. You're lying!

JIMMY. You don't tell a stranger about your former lover's taint tattoo. I was here when she died peacefully in her sleep.

RODNEY. But why are you doing this sick Norman Bates impersonation? Why are you wearing her clothes and her wig?

JIMMY. It's a long story. Suffice to say I'm posing as her. Can we leave it at that?

RODNEY. You tell me the whole story or I'll beat the crap out of you. When I'm finished nobody will recognize you as Adriana or even as human.

JIMMY. That's a terrible thing to say.

RODNEY. I am capable of extreme violence.

JIMMY. I refuse to believe that.

RODNEY. I've been arrested on numerous occasions for assault. The last time was when I broke the jaw of a salesman at Pottery Barn.

JIMMY. It's very irritating when nothing's in stock.

RODNEY. What the fuck's going on?

JIMMY. Okay. Just calm down. Rita and I –

RODNEY. She's in on it too?

JIMMY. She's my oldest friend. I rent a room here when I'm not performing in Vegas. We, Adriana, Rita and I, were drinking and camping around. Rita and I passed out and when we woke up, Adriana was dead. And we got this scheme that if we pinned a fake ID on her, I could pose as Adriana long enough for Rita to sell the house and we'd split the money.

RODNEY. You thought you'd get away with this?

JIMMY. We thought it was…fool proof. But then, get this, it turned out that the house was in her husband's name. Adriana could live in it till she died but he willed the house to his only living relative; his niece in Wisconsin.

RODNEY. That sour-faced chick I met earlier?

JIMMY. She thinks her Aunt is trying to bilk her out of her inheritance.

RODNEY. Is she stupid enough to believe that you're Adriana?

JIMMY. You believed it until you felt me up.

RODNEY. This is very interesting. Very interesting. *(He laughs to himself.)*

JIMMY. It is sort of kooky, isn't it?

RODNEY. How long have you been living as Adriana?

JIMMY. Oh, five weeks.

RODNEY. How do you pay her bills?

JIMMY. I found all her bank passwords and I just pay everything online. So you won't say anything?

RODNEY. I won't say anything, provided that –

JIMMY. Provided that I give you part of the money.

RODNEY. Part? All of the money.

JIMMY. Oh, come on. Play fair.

RODNEY. You will make sure that Christina splits the money with you and then you will give me your entire share or I'll report you to the police.

JIMMY. I thought you were a different person now. You said you regret all the nasty things you've done.

RODNEY. I have no regrets. I put out plenty to Adriana. That bitch got her money's worth out of me.

JIMMY. You're not grateful for everything she taught you?

RODNEY. She taught me to have contempt for any honest human emotion. Next to that monster I've always been a rank amateur. So game on. What do I call you? Miss Thing?

JIMMY. Jimmy.

RODNEY. Well, Jimmy, hand over those earrings. Are they real diamonds?

JIMMY. *(removing his earrings)* Not sure. Are these the earrings you put on when Adriana dressed you up in drag?

RODNEY. I've never been in drag.

JIMMY. Just five minutes ago –.

RODNEY. I never told you that.

JIMMY. What do you mean? You told me that –

RODNEY. I never told you that.

JIMMY. I'm sorry. I don't know where I got that idea.

RODNEY. Adriana had a vault in the cellar to store her furs. Is it still there?

JIMMY. It's still there.

RODNEY. Well, if you try anything funny, you'll end up in that vault.

JIMMY. I won't try anything funny. Rodney, so now that we're in business together, would that preclude any possibility of our being, um, intimate? You're a fabulous kisser.

RODNEY. Yes, it would. (**RODNEY** *takes out his iphone and takes photos of the room.*)

JIMMY. Why? I thought we had a real chemistry.

RODNEY. Because I'm not gay.

JIMMY. Not at all? It seemed like you were really into it.

RODNEY. Because I thought you were a woman. *(with an edge of threat)* I come off gay to you?

JIMMY. No. It's just that you seem like someone who explores all of life's possibilities.

RODNEY. Only with women. I've got a lot to do. I need to get this inventory appraised.

JIMMY. That's a big job.

RODNEY. That's why I'll be living here.

JIMMY. You'll be living here?

RODNEY. To keep an eye on all of you.

JIMMY. The Romanov bedroom on the third floor is lovely. Very private. But back to what I was saying.

RODNEY. I'm not interested in anything you have to say.

JIMMY. Stop that. Look. You can fool around with someone once and that wouldn't mean you were gay. And after you did it, you might just say, "That was fun but not for me." You might want to even try it a second time or

even a third time just to make absolutely sure it wasn't
for you.

RODNEY. Listen to these words. There are six of them.
I don't want to have sex with you.

JIMMY. Those are eight words.

RODNEY. I don't want to have sex with you. Yes, eight
words. And I'll add a ninth. "Ever."

JIMMY. What exactly are you saying?

RODNEY. I am not attracted to men. I have never had sex
with a man. I have no intention of having sex with a
man.

JIMMY. But —

RODNEY. You get Christina to split the money with you or
else I'll have you arrested. And don't even think of
telling your friend Rita that I'm onto you, if you value
your lives.

(**RODNEY** *exits through the front door.*)

JIMMY. I can't believe this is happening. *(with undiluted joy)*
I have a boyfriend!

End of Act One

ACT TWO

Scene One

*(Afternoon. **CHRISTINA** is dusting. Her arm is bandaged. **RITA** enters from upstairs. She's on her way to the office.)*

RITA. Every time I see you you're cleaning something.

CHRISTINA. When you live in a dump like I do, the only thing you can do is keep it spotless.

RITA. Paulina was just here yesterday. She's new. Is there something she's not doing?

CHRISTINA. She's fine. I'm just nuts. I sweep under rugs. I wash all the glassware every week. That way I don't have to think about the future.

RITA. What happened to your arm?

CHRISTINA. I don't want to sound overly dramatic, but this morning, I barely escaped the jaws of death.

RITA. You got my attention.

CHRISTINA. I was going to do a load of laundry and when I started down the steps to the cellar, one of the steps cracked right from under me. Thank God I was holding on to the railing.

RITA. That's terrible.

CHRISTINA. I could have broken my neck. As it is, my whole spine feels out of alignment. Of course, I'm not surprised this happened. I'm the center of a negative force field.

RITA. Christina – .

CHRISTINA. A radioactive cloud of misfortune follows me everywhere, from Milwaukee to the Big Apple.

RITA. *(puts her bag down)* Christina, the future doesn't have to be so bleak if you'd just let me sell the goddam house. The future could be very rosy indeed.

CHRISTINA. Well, you've certainly got me over a barrel. My problems are over if I agree to split the money. And if I don't, I have to wait until Aunt Adriana drops dead. And frankly, she's looking younger and juicier every day.

RITA. Loneliness is aging. She likes having you guys around. Where are they now?

CHRISTINA. She took him to another old movie at the museum. It was so much easier for me when I could simply hate her like a Disney villainess. But she's been so damned delightful. She makes me feel guilty for hating her and I will not feel guilty. I am the injured party.

RITA. She's mellowed. Take it from me. She is definitely not the woman she was.

CHRISTINA. I'd also like to believe that you and I are getting along and you don't have an ulterior motive. I was prepared to despise you.

RITA. Oh, you made that very clear. I don't want to be on your enemies list.

CHRISTINA. I was pretty worked up when we first got here.

RITA. Worked up? You were in a frenzy. You terrified me.

CHRISTINA. No, I didn't.

RITA. Christina, for the first week you were here, I was walking on eggshells. You were very intimidating.

CHRISTINA. Really? I was intimidating. That's the nicest thing anyone has ever said to me.

RITA. You regarded us with utter contempt.

CHRISTINA. What was I to think? Imagine if you were me.

RITA. I told Adriana that any further discussion was futile. There was no way you would ever consider splitting the money.

CHRISTINA. Well, if I had to make a decision this very minute, I'd take the risk and wait till Aunt Adriana croaks and get the whole amount.

RITA. That's your decision. There's not much I can do to dissuade you. You're a woman of strong convictions.

CHRISTINA. I am? Say that again.

RITA. You're a woman of strong convictions.

CHRISTINA. I love this. Now say it in a different way.

RITA. You're a woman who adamantly adheres to her own sense of – what do you think I'm Roget's Thesaurus?

(They both laugh. RODNEY comes in from the kitchen. He's barely suppressing his cold rage.)

RODNEY. Did either of you clean out the refrigerator?

CHRISTINA. I wiped it down this morning.

RODNEY. Did you open my bag of food?

CHRISTINA. No. Of course not.

RODNEY. It looks tampered with.

CHRISTINA. *(intimidated)* I swear I didn't. I put the bag on the counter while I cleaned and then I put it back.

RODNEY. Just don't touch my food. Okay? I don't ask for much. Am I making myself clear?

RITA. You're making it perfectly clear that you're something of a lunatic. Nobody is going to open your bag of groceries, if your name's on it.

RODNEY. I'm sorry if I sounded antagonistic. It's a sensitive issue for me.

RITA. Evidently. This is something you should deal with in counseling.

RODNEY. I'll take that under consideration.

CHRISTINA. We all have our idiosyncrasies.

RITA. Naturally, you've raised our suspicions. What could be in that bag that's of such vital concern to you?

RODNEY. I'm macro-biotic. I nearly died from abusing my body and now I have this obsession that everything I ingest be pure and clean. A while back, I was working for – well, without breaching security, let's just say, I was contracted by a covert government agency. We were investigating a drug cartel in Bolivia and I was sent undercover. A few months into it, I was ratted on by one of my own superiors. I was blindfolded and driven into the mountains in the trunk of a car. My clothes were torn off me and I was pinned naked to the ground by strips of barbed wire. To get information out of me, I was force fed contaminated raw chicken heads. The bastards got nothing out of me but puke…for seventy two hours. I was close to death from dehydration when I was finally rescued in a bloody ambush. That should explain my finicky eating habits.

CHRISTINA. Wow.

RODNEY. Hey, what happened to your arm?

CHRISTINA. One of the steps going down to the cellar broke right from under me.

RODNEY. You could have been killed.

CHRISTINA. It was a close call. We need to get it fixed.

RODNEY. I'll get on it. There are a lot of things that ought to be repaired if you intend to sell this place.

RITA. The place is fine. We *had* a buyer. These village townhouses go very quickly.

RODNEY. You've sold high end properties before?

RITA. Yes, I have.

RODNEY. You have?

RITA. You seem skeptical.

RODNEY. I'm assuming you're living here rent free. Therefore my next assumption is that you can't afford to live on your own, so I can only assume you're not doing too well in the real estate biz.

RITA. Well, your assumptions are wrong. I can afford my own apartment. Adriana and I are friends who enjoy living together and caring for each other. *You* seem very comfortable here.

RODNEY. It's almost as if I've never been away.

RITA. Picking up from where you left off?

RODNEY. We're much older now. Adriana's become more of a mother figure to me.

CHRISTINA. I think she looks twenty years younger than her age.

RODNEY. Christina, after all you've been through, you're still a romantic. But I'm afraid I have to disappoint you. Adriana and I are keeping it strictly platonic. In fact, she'd like nothing more than to see me fall in love. Now if you ladies will excuse me.

(**RODNEY** *goes upstairs.*)

CHRISTINA. I hate to say it but I find him unbelievably sexy. I dunno. There's something very vulnerable about him.

RITA. You see vulnerable. I see shifty.

CHRISTINA. What do I know? Back home I had an unrequited sexual obsession with the mailman. A tall, hunched over beanpole with the most soulful melancholy eyes. My best friend Melanie thinks I just desperately need to get laid.

RITA. Has it been awhile?

CHRISTINA. I have not had sex in…let me think about it for a second. Five years. That includes the last three years of my marriage. Melanie was very wise.

RITA. She's the one who died this year?

CHRISTINA. Yeah. We were incredibly close. Some people at work thought we were lovers.

RITA. And you never were?

CHRISTINA. Oh God, no. Not that there is anything wrong with being gay.

RITA. You don't have to be politically correct with me.

CHRISTINA. I'm not. I've just never been so aware of homophobia as I've been during these past two years. I want to do everything possible to make life smoother for my kid but mostly I fail. She's flunking all her classes. Her teachers have totally given up on her. And there's a limit to what I can do. I can't afford special tutors. And I was totally unscholastic so I can't work with her. I'm worthless. I'm still calling him "she." I can't even get my pronouns correct.

RITA. Ouch.

CHRISTINA. I guess I'm a little hard on myself.

RITA. Yeah. I'd say so.

CHRISTINA. You seem very comfortable with who you are; as a lesbian and a broker. I truly believe that all people are in some degree bisexual.

RITA. So what degree are you?

CHRISTINA. I've never had a lesbian experience so maybe six per cent going to seven. I wouldn't be surprised if someday a gay woman with a strong personality has her way with me. Seriously, I'm holding on to heterosexuality with white knuckles. My track record with men is disastrous.

RITA. Every relationship of mine ends with bitter recrimination and a broken knick knack. The bottom line is I drink too much.

CHRISTINA. Are you still drinking?

RITA. I've promised Jimmy I wouldn't.

CHRISTINA. Who's Jimmy? I've heard you mention him a couple of times.

RITA. A friend of ours. Anyway, I promised I'd abstain from all alcoholic beverages and I'm doing very well. But I'm sure I'll end my days as a hopeless drunk.

CHRISTINA. You sound so fatalistic.

RITA. I'm a realist. I can see my future mapped out. I'll be living in some place like Key West. I'll be a local character. Beloved by some, reviled by others. Over tanned...emaciated. I'll be a fixture at some gay bar. Or maybe a talent booker for the disco. People will say "There's no point in doing business with Rita after four pm. She's too far gone. Incoherent." I'll have an entourage of young gay boys who will carry me up the stairs after happy hour to my room above the bar and put me to bed. I'll be lucky to have them because I'll have alienated everyone else with my vicious alcoholic ravings. When I drink I'm a truth teller. A Cassandra. I frighten people with my scalding observations. I've been called "unbearable." Oh yeah, to my face. Unbearable. Obnoxious. Caustic. Loud.

(**RITA** *notices that* **CHRISTINA** *has settled into a strange dark mood.*)

RITA. I think I've depressed you.

CHRISTINA. No, you haven't.

RITA. I can tell by your eyes that you've gone to some very dark place.

CHRISTINA. I guess I have. I'm sorry. It's not you.

RITA. Well, what's going on?

CHRISTINA. I miss my friend Melanie. If only she was alive. I wish I could call her right now.

RITA. Unfinished business?

CHRISTINA. No.

RITA. A confession?

CHRISTINA. Yeah.

RITA. How terrible can it be?

CHRISTINA. It's bad.

RITA. Well, can you pretend that you're talking to Melanie?

CHRISTINA. I'm not good at that sort of thing. I really can't talk about it.

RITA. Hey, Christina. It's me, Mel. I got this sudden feeling that you really needed to talk to me.

CHRISTINA. I can't do this.

RITA. I promise I won't tell anyone. Jackie Kennedy is right over here and she never blabs.

CHRISTINA. Oh Melanie. I did a terrible thing.

RITA. I bet it's not nearly as awful as you think.

CHRISTINA. When you died, I was sitting by your bedside. I'm sorry I can't do this.

RITA. Come on. You're almost there.

CHRISTINA. I held your hand and watched you slip away. We were all alone. The room became so still. You were gone. Then I let go of your hand and I walked over to your dresser. I was sort of on auto pilot. I'd like to think I was looking for the hospitals' phone number. But maybe I wasn't. Maybe I was looking for your wallet because that's what I found in the top drawer. I took out your Visa and your Mastercard. I put them in my bag. I'm broke. I've been living off these stolen credit cards but at the end of the month when the bills come in, your husband's going to figure it out. I'm so scared. I'm so scared.

Scene Two

*(The following night. **JIMMY** is lying on the sofa reading a book. He's wearing his **ADRIANA** wig but his regular jeans and an untucked man's button down shirt. **RODNEY** comes down the stairs holding a set of legal documents.)*

RODNEY. We need to talk.

(He closes the pocket doors.)

JIMMY. Well, we could discuss literature. Ever read De Maupassant? I found this on the bookcase.

RODNEY. Why are you dressed like a guy?

JIMMY. Because Adriana is a lady who likes to be comfortable.

RODNEY. Adriana never wore jeans.

JIMMY. Well, I am my own Adriana.

RODNEY. What the hell does that mean?

JIMMY. Christina only met her once when she was ten years old. That leaves me a lot of…wiggle room.

RODNEY. One of these days Nutso and the kid are going to see through your act. If you blow it, I'd still turn you in.

JIMMY. Posing as another person is not as easy as people think. You ought to know that.

RODNEY. What's that supposed to mean?

JIMMY. I'm referring to your experience as a faux physician in charge of medical cadavers.

RODNEY. I don't know what you're talking about.

JIMMY. In Romania, when you were selling body parts.

RODNEY. I never did that.

JIMMY. Sorry. I must be confusing you with some other free-lance body organ peddler.

RODNEY. I want you to sign these papers.

JIMMY. What kind of papers?

RODNEY. You're giving me power of attorney.

JIMMY. That's not necessary.

RODNEY. Just shut up and sign 'em. *(He hands the papers to* **JIMMY**.*)*

JIMMY. I've never had to sign a single thing as Adriana. That's all I need is to be accused of forgery.

RODNEY. You're different tonight.

JIMMY. Maybe I'm getting over my attraction to you. Perhaps your rudeness is becoming something of a bore.

RODNEY. You're over me, huh?

JIMMY. It's hard sustaining a crush on a blank wall.

RODNEY. You think I'm a blank wall? Have you ever wondered how I got that tattoo on my upper taint?

JIMMY. Upper taint. That's somewhere in Westchester. Isn't it?

RODNEY. I was seventeen. My junkie Mom was writhing on the kitchen floor in withdrawal. She begged me to go into the city and get her some smack. I told her I couldn't do it, but she grabbed a carving knife and threatened to slit her throat. So I took the car and found the address of her connection. Inside were three black dudes who were very surprised to see me. It seems that Ma had forgotten that she owed these gentlemen over five hundred bucks. The tallest of the three slammed me against the concrete wall. They took out their guns and forced me to strip naked. I blacked out. When I came to, I was lying in a back alley. I felt this excruciating pain between my legs. I checked it out and saw that they had tattooed me so I wouldn't forget. And even though I've had it for over thirty years, I don't know what the symbol means.

JIMMY. Well, why don't you let me take a look at it? Maybe a fresh pair of eyes.

RODNEY. I'll pass on that suggestion.

JIMMY. You're really somethin'. You hand out these wild stories about yourself and yet they don't really tell me anything. Who are you?

RODNEY. Just a guy who stumbled onto a jackpot when he landed in this house.

JIMMY. And people accuse me of acting like I'm in an old movie. For one moment could you just be for real?

RODNEY. I am totally "for real."

JIMMY. Do you like lobster?

RODNEY. Do I like lobster? Is that a euphemism?

JIMMY. Absolutely not. I really want to know. Do you like eating lobster? I could eat a pound and a quarter lobster every day of my life.

RODNEY. I haven't eaten a lobster in many years.

JIMMY. But when you did eat lobster, did you like it steamed or broiled?

RODNEY. I can't remember. Where are you going with this?

JIMMY. Do you like the kitchen breaking it up for you, or do you like cracking it yourself?

RODNEY. This conversation is irrelevant. I eat what's necessary to live.

JIMMY. Let me try something else.

RODNEY. No.

(He starts to leave. **JIMMY** *crosses and blocks the door.)*

JIMMY. What's your favorite song?

RODNEY. I don't listen to music. Get away from those doors.

JIMMY. Do you like to sleep?

RODNEY. I keep one eye open.

JIMMY. Do you dream? Tell me a dream.

RODNEY. I will never discuss my dreams with anyone. Least of all you.

JIMMY. What are your bathroom habits like?

RODNEY. What?

JIMMY. Tell me about your bathroom habits?

RODNEY. You're out of your mind.

JIMMY. It's a basic function of life. Do you relax and read the paper while you're on the pot?

RODNEY. No. I get in and out quickly.

JIMMY. Do you flush right away or do you take a quick look in the bowl to see how you did?

RODNEY. Is this sort of your kink?

JIMMY. I just want you to be "you." So? Do you?

RODNEY. No, I don't look at it. I get out of there.

JIMMY. You get out of there? It's a place of privacy.

RODNEY. I don't like going to the bathroom.

JIMMY. You don't like it?

RODNEY. I don't even like peeing. I've trained myself to go twelve hours without taking a piss.

JIMMY. That's not good. You'll get kidney stones.

RODNEY. Okay. I've indulged your warped fantasies.

JIMMY. I'm serious. I want you to promise me that you'll drink at least three tumblers of water every day and urinate freely. Will you promise me that?

RODNEY. You don't care about me. I know what you want and you're not going to get it. Did you ever think that I might seduce Christina? She's very hot for me, you know. With very little effort, I could get that stupid bitch to marry me and you'd be totally out of the picture. I might even murder you in your sleep and make it look like a suicide so there are no loose ends. That's a simple pleasure I could really get into.

(**RODNEY** *opens one of the pocket doors. He crosses to the front door and exits.*)

JIMMY. Ohhhh, he's so cute.

(**RACHEL,** *who has been hiding in the corner of the foyer, enters the sitting room.*)

RACHEL. Aunt Adriana, are you all right?

JIMMY. Of course, I am. Why shouldn't I be?

RACHEL. I wasn't spying. I wanted to say good night and I overheard Rodney saying those horrible things just now.

JIMMY. What exactly did you hear?

RACHEL. That he could get Mom to marry him and that he would kill you.

JIMMY. Oh that. *(laughs gaily)*

RACHEL. I didn't think it was funny.

JIMMY. But it was! *C'est drole*! Rodney's a frustrated actor. We improvise old movie scenes together, but we're not always in the same movie.

RACHEL. He really scares me.

JIMMY. Darling, your voice is going up again. Try again and don't be afraid of raising your volume.

RACHEL. *(making her voice too deep)* He really scares me.

JIMMY. Let's do the exercise.

(**RACHEL** *sings a scale from her middle register down to a very low tone.*)

JIMMY. Now find the middle.

RACHEL. *(finding a naturally male tone)* He really scares me.

JIMMY. Perfection. Has Rodney said anything to you?

RACHEL. It's the whole picture. What's all that about not touching any of his food in the refrigerator?

JIMMY. He's lived in homeless shelters where he had to protect his possessions. And I think something really terrible happened to him when he was a child.

RACHEL. He still doesn't have to be so obnoxious.

JIMMY. I shouldn't be telling you this but a few years ago, he was abducted in Romania and forced to impersonate a doctor who sold body parts commercially.

RACHEL. He was forced to do this?

JIMMY. Or he would have been killed.

RACHEL. I'm not buying it.

JIMMY. Not buying it? That's an odd reaction, I must say.

RACHEL. If it is true, you don't think he's still in business, do you?

JIMMY. No. The man's as scrupulously honest as I am. I had to travel to Romania and employ all my husband's diplomatic contacts to smuggle him out of the country. *(emotionally)* When I found him he was near death. I nursed him back to health on a goat farm in a small village outside Zurich.

RACHEL. But I thought you hadn't seen Rodney in over twenty years.

JIMMY. Well, this was just a brief episode. Once I knew he was safe and in good health, I bid him farewell and resolved never to see him again. And didn't until you brought him back to me.

RACHEL. Are you still lovers?

JIMMY. Pitch.

RACHEL. Don't use my voice lessons to evade the question.

JIMMY. Yes, we are. Our lovemaking has remained passionate, creative and tender.

RACHEL. Can I ask you a very, very, very personal question?

JIMMY. Can it just be a very, very personal question?

RACHEL. It's something I've been wondering about since the first day we got here. And I think I know the answer.

JIMMY. Close the doors.

> (**RACHEL** *closes the pocket doors.*)

JIMMY. Yeah?

RACHEL. *(pause)* Are you transgender?

JIMMY. *(shocked)* Am I what?

RACHEL. Were you born a biological male?

JIMMY. *(at a loss)* Why would you ask me that?

RACHEL. It's obviously something I'm very attuned to and something important to me. Well, are you?

JIMMY. Yes.

RACHEL. Did your husband know?

JIMMY. He was a very worldly man and loved me unconditionally.

RACHEL. Did any of your friends or business associates know?

JIMMY. It was our secret. I've never discussed this with anyone.

RACHEL. I promise I won't tell a soul. How awful to live like that. But obviously Rodney knows.

JIMMY. Yes. Rodney knows. I did everything I could to discourage him. But there was an almost cataclysmic sexual chemistry between us from the start.

RACHEL. He seems so straight.

JIMMY. He is straight. But somehow I'm the big exception.

RACHEL. I can't believe I'm having this conversation with my Great Aunt. Tell me again you're not in any danger. If anything happened to you, *(She clings to* JIMMY.*)* I couldn't stand it. I really couldn't.

JIMMY. Oh my. Oh my. Nothing's going to happen to me. I may come off rather delicate but I'm much tougher than people think.

(There is a knock on the pocket door.)

JIMMY. Yes?

(CHRISTINA opens the door and enters.)

CHRISTINA. Why are these doors shut? I'm not intruding on anything personal, am I?

JIMMY. Not at all, my dear. Not at all. The child and I were simply planning our next adventure. Cherie, how is your arm?

CHRISTINA. Much better. And I can move my head almost all around. It's always something with me. I basically escape death four times a day.

JIMMY. Well, you got through today without a disaster.

CHRISTINA. Barely.

RACHEL. What's happened now?

CHRISTINA. It's so embarrassing. I was taking my vitamins this morning. I take about twenty of 'em. My one luxury and I buy 'em dirt cheap from Canada. So I have this ritual. I line up the vitamins on the counter and then make a clean sweep with my hand and swallow them all together. Well, this morning, I almost accidentally swallowed a thumb tack.

RACHEL. Didn't you check to see if the counter top was clean?

CHRISTINA. I thought I did. It was a very tiny tack. I obviously didn't see it.

RACHEL. Are you sure the tack wasn't in one of your vitamin bottles? Was it a new bottle?

CHRISTINA. No.

RACHEL. So it was already open. Someone could have put the tack in there.

CHRISTINA. Please don't turn this into a conspiracy.

RACHEL. First you're nearly killed when the cellar step breaks under you and now you swallow a thumb tack.

CHRISTINA. I'm accident prone. From now on I'll take my vitamins like a normal person.

(**RITA** *enters through the front door. She's been drinking but it manifests itself in loud egomania and not slurred sloppiness.*)

RITA. Hey, I thought you'd all be in bed.

JIMMY. You're out very late.

RITA. I was with friends.

JIMMY. At the Cubby hole?

RITA. As a matter of fact I was.

CHRISTINA. What's the Cubby Hole?

RACHEL. A woman's bar. And no, Mom, I haven't been there. I've only heard about it.

RITA. And I'm pleased to report that I imbibed only diet coke. I went to the Cubby Hole to celebrate.

RACHEL. You have good news?

RITA. Well, hold onto your teeth, kids. After I left work this afternoon I passed by that eyesore of a dilapidated townhouse on Barrow Street that's been for sale for the past millennium. That evil twat Celeste is the broker. She's like the negative version of me. As fate would have it, today was the open house. I saunter in very nonchalantly just as Celeste and her potential buyers are traipsing through Hell House. I recognized this woman, Evelyn, the wife of a fabulously wealthy hedge funder, lingering by the dumbwaiter. I seize the moment! When no one is looking, I edge over to her and say without any rancor, "Can you believe what that Celeste is trying to get for this shit hole?" Evelyn concurred that the place had no pizazz, no je ne sais quoi and no moldings. Contrary to what my enemies might say, I am a brilliant broker. I paint a picture. I give my clients a glimpse of a glorious future. Can we just say it? I am an artist!

JIMMY. Get to the point. And?

RITA. So I tell her "You're looking for a one family townhouse? I got one. Wedding cake ceilings, French doors, backyard garden." When I told her about the skylight on the top floor, she started frothing at the mouth. Frothing like a mad dog. She's willing to drop fifteen million for the right property. I might be able to start even higher. Christina, would you please say something?

CHRISTINA. That's great but I don't know what I want to do. I'm still very confused.

RITA. There's nothing confusing about fifteen million dollars.

CHRISTINA. I haven't made up my mind about anything.

RITA. What's to make up? You're either rolling in dough or waiting for *this* bitch to kick the bucket.

JIMMY. Rita, don't badger her.

RITA. I just don't understand this dilly dallying. The market is very capricious. This could be it.

JIMMY. Darling, you've been consuming more than diet coke. I think you should go to bed.

RITA. I couldn't agree more. I need to be with people who make decisions. Movers and shakers!

(*She moves towards the stairs and trips.* **CHRISTINA** *gasps.*)

JIMMY. Oliver, would you see that the poor beast gets up the stairs?

RITA. I do not need assistance.

RACHEL. I'm going up anyway.

JIMMY. Good night, my dear. (*JIMMY kisses* **RACHEL.**)

RACHEL. Good night, Mom.

(**CHRISTINA** *hugs her closely.*)

CHRISTINA. You're my one bit of good luck.

RITA. (*shaking off* **RACHEL**'s *grip on her arm*) Peter Pan, I can fly to Neverland on my own accord.

(*The two of them go upstairs.*)

CHRISTINA. No one's trying to kill me, are they?

JIMMY. Who would want to kill you?

CHRISTINA. You and Rita. I'm keeping you from selling this house and fifteen million dollars. Let's be honest. I am the type who ends up murdered. I'm in the way. I've always been in the way. I was in my parents' way. They were so in love. They would have been much happier without children. I was in my husband's way and he got out. Oliver needs me but in a few years, he'll want to be on his own and I'll be in *his* way.

JIMMY. Well, darling, everyone's in somebody's way.

CHRISTINA. But I'm *always* in the way. Sincerely, more people accidentally bump into me on the street than is the norm. I'm perpetually bruised. Fate has turned me into this sad sack bore. You're such a free spirit. When have you been at your lowest ebb?

JIMMY. I'm there.

CHRISTINA. Doesn't Rodney living here make it any better?

JIMMY. You'd think. But he's a complicated fellow. I seem to have a predilection for shmucks. I know from the start that they're going to treat me badly. And when they do, it's almost a relief.

CHRISTINA. Aunt Adriana, it's the oddest thing. Your accent sort of comes and goes. Sometimes you sound completely American.

JIMMY. Well, I have lived in this country for over fifty years. I suppose at this point, the accent is more of an affectation.

CHRISTINA. I like it when you're – unaffected. Can I – cuddle with you for a minute? I can't remember the last time anyone held me. Please?

JIMMY. Okay.

(**CHRISTINA** *curls up next to* **JIMMY** *on the sofa, with her head against him.*)

CHRISTINA. This was always my big fantasy. I wanted you to hold me and tell me I was pretty. I sort of understand why you didn't take to me as a child. I was so dull and awkward and ugly. I haven't really changed.

JIMMY. So we're going down that path again, are we?

CHRISTINA. I guess I'm passable but I really don't like my looks at all.

JIMMY. *(as Bette Davis)* But who wants that kind of prettiness, Tina? There's something else you can have, if you earn it. A kind of beauty. A light that shines from inside you, because you're a nice person. In the meantime, if it helps, I like you and I think you're very pretty, very sweet.

CHRISTINA. Are you doing Bette Davis?

JIMMY. No.

CHRISTINA. I've seen this movie on TV. She's a fat spinster and she goes on a cruise and comes back skinny and with her eyebrows tweezed. And she has an affair with a married man and then takes care of his homely daughter.

JIMMY. *Now Voyager.* Although I'm not sure I'd go with that synopsis.

CHRISTINA. So you are doing her.

JIMMY. *(very uncomfortable)* Yeah.

CHRISTINA. Why do you do that? Am I being too emotional? It makes you nervous?

JIMMY. I suppose. I don't know.

CHRISTINA. I want to get through to you, but it's like you're wearing a Halloween mask.

JIMMY. I'm really not wearing a mask. I mean it's incredible how much of a mask I'm not wearing.

CHRISTINA. If you had to paint an honest picture of yourself… No, this is better. If you had to shoot a one minute video that would absolutely define you, what would it be?

JIMMY. Where do you come up with these things? A one minute video? Let's see… Well, I guess I'd be walking by myself down a very windy street. Kind of grim, isn't it?

CHRISTINA. I could have been a comfort to you. Why were you so mean to me when I came here to visit?

JIMMY. What do you want me to say? I resented having you here. I wanted to be alone with my husband.

CHRISTINA. You really loved Uncle Lou?

JIMMY. I adored him. You must remember he was much older than me. He was like both a father and a husband. And of course he was the polar opposite of my own *Papa*. Lou was a brilliant man, a diplomat and my father had an unsuccessful lamp store.

CHRISTINA. In Europe.

JIMMY. Vienna. The winters were so lovely. The powdery snow covering the Wienerwald.

CHRISTINA. Oh, so then you were living in Austria during World War Two?

JIMMY. *(madly inventing)* We had to escape. We had to flee on a midnight train, passports purloined on the black market. Think *Three Comrades. The Mortal Storm*. Margaret Sullavan. My father moved the lamps, everything to Sweden. Stockholm.

CHRISTINA. But when you were in Vienna, did you see –

JIMMY. I don't even remember Vienna. I was so young and traumatized. Anyway, it was a magical kind of store, all amber light and crystal beading on the lampshades, right out of *The Shop Around the Corner*. A 1940 Lubitsch comedy. Margaret Sullavan was in that one too. Well, you don't make a killing selling finials on the fjord.

But that didn't stop my father from having a wild old time, particularly after my mother died. He was more like a younger brother than a father.

CHRISTINA. Uncle Lou was more of a father to me than my own dad. He was the only person who seemed truly interested in everything I had to say.

JIMMY. I wouldn't call my father a listener. But when he was around, he was a lot of fun. And he could be very affectionate. I used to sleepwalk when I was little and they'd always find me curled up in the laundry basket in the linen closet holding his shirt collar close to my nose. There was something about the cool crispness of the collar and the clean smell of the starch that I loved. Maybe it was just him.

CHRISTINA. I would have saved one of those shirts.

JIMMY. I didn't. At a certain point I had to cut him out of my life. You just couldn't depend on him. I once developed a terrible sty on my eye. The kind that won't go away by itself. It had to be operated on but he couldn't get around to making the appointment for the surgery. It kept getting bigger and bigger and became sort of carnival side show freakish. Finally a teacher of mine contacted someone from the Child Welfare Department, who had to step in and set up the appointment to remove the chalazion, that's what they call it, and then make sure my father took me there. So at twelve years old, I decided to live with my grandmother…in Lisbon. I wanted to. I had to. He was fun but dangerous. Later on, when I was grown up…and working in Paris, my father tried very hard to make amends. He seemed grateful for any bone I threw at him. He was very proud of what I'd done with my life. Surprising, considering my profession. You know, fashion. I wanted to be affectionate with him and sort of faked it. You see I can just turn off all feeling like a light switch. Maybe that's my one minute video self-portrait. Me turning off the light switch on a beautiful but highly impractical antique lamp.

CHRISTINA. My video would be me going into my best friend Melanie's drawer as soon as she was dead and stealing her Visa and Mastercards. Because that's what I did and that's what I've been living on.

JIMMY. You did that?

CHRISTINA. You sound almost pleased. I'm gonna be caught. The police will trace the charges.

JIMMY. Well, have you been photographed by surveillance cameras when you've bought things?

CHRISTINA. I always wore a wig. I'm a hairdresser. I'm good with wigs.

JIMMY. Didn't you have to show a picture ID?

CHRISTINA. I also stole her driver's license. We resemble each other. We could have been sisters.

JIMMY. Did you pay for your plane tickets with the stolen card?

CHRISTINA. Yes. Online.

JIMMY. Well, maybe you won't be caught. People do get away with crazy things sometimes.

CHRISTINA. You know, you don't act like an old lady. I hope you won't mind me saying this but you'd look a lot younger with a different wig. At least a different style.

JIMMY. You don't think it's attractive?

CHRISTINA. It's all right, but have you ever thought about going shorter? More layered? Kind of like Marilyn.

JIMMY. Oh, no, not Marilyn. Besides this look has been my trademark.

CHRISTINA. Well, maybe it's time to shake things up. Let me wash and style it for you? Add some color. This is what I do. I want to please you. It'll be my gift.

JIMMY. That's all right.

CHRISTINA. Come on. Don't be afraid.

*(She pulls off **JIMMY**'s wig. She's oblivious to his maleness. She looks at the label on the wig.)*

CHRISTINA. This is a good wig. I've got my second wind. I'm going to wash and cut it right now. And tomorrow I'll get some curlers and set it and I can have it ready for you by tomorrow night. Do you have a second wig to wear?

JIMMY. No. So hand it over.

(**CHRISTINA** *hands him the wig, and* **JIMMY** *plops it back on his head.*)

CHRISTINA. Let's go upstairs. I have a terrycloth turban you can wear. Come on. This is going to be fun. Wait till Rodney sees you with your new look. He'll flip.

(**CHRISTINA** *goes up the stairs.* **JIMMY** *turns out all the lights but one and follows her up the stairs. The house settles into night. The front door opens and* **RODNEY** *comes back carrying with great effort a large garment bag filled with what seems like a dead body. He accidentally knocks over a lamp. He puts down the body and puts the lamp back on the table.* **RACHEL***, hearing the noise, comes out of her upstairs room and sees him carrying the body towards the kitchen and thus to the cellar.*)

Scene Three

(The following night. **RODNEY** *and* **CHRISTINA** *are dancing a sexy Rhumba.* **RITA**, *in her pajamas and a bathrobe, is on the sofa, nursing a drink. A plate of salami is on a table.)*

CHRISTINA. We've waited so long to have any fun together. Why have we spent every evening alone in our separate cells?

RODNEY. We've been feeling each other out.

CHRISTINA. That sounds kind of nasty.

RODNEY. You bring in out in me. Stop being such a bad influence.

CHRISTINA. I love being a bad influence.

RITA. We should keep it down. We don't want to wake up the kid.

CHRISTINA. He's a very sound sleeper. Tonight I'm uncensored!

(After getting **CHRISTINA** *all hot and bothered,* **RODNEY** *breaks away from her and turns down the portable CD player.)*

RODNEY. Maybe we *should* lower the volume. *(He closes the pocket door.)* We don't want to disturb Adriana. I think she's sleeping.

(He moves in to kiss **CHRISTINA**. *Nervously, she pulls away.)*

CHRISTINA. Are you kidding? Adriana's the original party girl.

RITA. Christina, sit here next to me.

CHRISTINA. You think I'm tanked. But I'm just feeling a kind of epic release. I've been under so much stress. For months. Years. But especially this past month.

RODNEY. This whole thing with the house?

CHRISTINA. That's the least of it.

RITA. *(changing the subject quickly)* But you've had some good times in New York. We should get out more while you're here.

CHRISTINA. Rodney, I've been living extremely close to the edge.

RODNEY. That's not such a bad thing. I'd encourage you to go further. Fall off.

CHRISTINA. *(to **RODNEY**)* What would you say if I told you that I stole my dead friend's credit cards?

RITA. She's putting us on.

CHRISTINA. I did steal my friend's credit cards. Mastercard and Visa.

RODNEY. No one's reported them missing?

CHRISTINA. Not yet. And let 'em try getting back her driver's license and social security card. Oops.

RODNEY. Have you told Adriana about this?

CHRISTINA. Last night.

RITA. Maybe you shouldn't tell any more people.

CHRISTINA. I just can't bear carrying the heavy weight of this secret.

RODNEY. I'm glad you're confiding in Adriana. She's a good listener.

CHRISTINA. I am feeling closer to her.

RODNEY. Have you thought any more about splitting the money with her?

CHRISTINA. You certainly cut to the chase.

RODNEY. It's hard to avoid. It's on all of our minds.

RITA. Why should it be on *your* mind?

RODNEY. I want them both to be happy and financially secure.

RITA. That's heartwarming.

RODNEY. Rita, you just don't like me, do you?

RITA. Sorry.

RODNEY. Well, maybe you're right. I consider it a miracle that Adriana has forgiven me.

CHRISTINA. You've changed.

RODNEY. No, I'm rotten to the core.

CHRISTINA. You're going to make me cry.

RODNEY. Well, are you thinking of splitting the money with her? I know Adriana's feeling a lot of anxiety about what you're going to do.

RITA. She's told you this?

RODNEY. Yes, she has. And at her age, that kind of tension isn't good. You don't want her blood pressure to sky rocket.

RITA. Leave her alone! My God you're annoying.

RODNEY. I'm not gonna sit back and passively watch Adriana have a stroke.

RITA. She is not going to have a stroke and you should just butt out.

RODNEY. Rita, maybe it's about time you didn't let your anti-male lesbian bias get in the way of your judgment.

RITA. I am not anti-male. I am anti-shit head.

CHRISTINA. We were having such a good time. Come on. Play nice.

RODNEY. I'm just very concerned about Adriana. She puts on a big show of strength and vitality. But she's really very fragile.

(**JIMMY** *shouts offstage, "Hit it!"* **CHRISTINA** *who hits "play" on the CD player.* **JIMMY** *enters in lounging pajamas, a feathered trimmed chiffon negligee and his new shorter fluffy hairstyle, looking a lot like Marilyn Monroe. He bursts into his Marilyn singing impersonation and uses* **RODNEY** *as a sexy prop.*)

JIMMY. *(sings)*
RUNNIN' WILD, LOST CONTROL
RUNNIN' WILD, MIGHTY BOLD
FEELIN' GAY, RECKLESS TOO
CAREFREE MIND ALL THE TIME, NEVER BLUE
ALWAYS GOING, DON'T KNOW WHERE
ALWAYS SHOWING. I DON'T CARE
DON'T LOVE NOBODY. IT'S NOT WORTHWHILE
ALL ALONE. RUNNING WILD!

CHRISTINA. You look fantastic! I did her hair! Doesn't she look great?

RODNEY. Unbelievable.

RITA. I believe it.

JIMMY. *(as Marilyn)* It's a new Adriana. Rita, you should let Christina take a crack at you.

CHRISTINA. No appointment necessary. That's a great Marilyn. You can do so many different voices.

JIMMY. It's a gift. I've always been mad for impressionists, especially female impersonators. Whenever Lou and I would go to any city, on our first night we'd find the local drag show.

RITA. Who wants another drink?

JIMMY. Rita, don't go overboard. You'll get tipsy. I've always been mad for female impersonators. Lou and I made the trek to Las Vegas almost every year to see this one glorious fellow who did Marilyn and Bette Davis and a million other women. Oh, he was brilliant. Such charisma. Such style. His name was Jimmy something or other.

CHRISTINA. Rita, is that the Jimmy that you sometimes mention?

RITA. No. That's a different Jimmy. I don't know this one.

(**JIMMY** *sits on* **RODNEY**'s *lap.*)

RODNEY. Are you comfortable?

JIMMY. Extremely. Let's liven things up. How about a party game? I've got a good one. We'll go around the room and tell each person which part of their body we like best.

RITA, RODNEY & CHRISTINA. No.

JIMMY. I'll go first. Rita has the most beautiful skin. And she does almost nothing to take care of it. It's real beautiful Irish Italian skin. Christina, touch her cheek. Isn't it heavenly?

(**CHRISTINA** *strokes* **RITA**'s *cheek.*)

CHRISTINA. Soft as silk.

JIMMY. And Christina, you have gorgeous eyes.

CHRISTINA. When I was a kid, you said I had pig eyes.

JIMMY. I was the jealous evil queen in Snow White. But your eyes are a remarkable color.

RODNEY. They seem to change according to your mood.

CHRISTINA. What color are they now?

RODNEY. A kind of blue green. With little flicks of hazel. Like a Siamese cat. Don't hypnotize me.

JIMMY. Hey! Back to me. It's still my turn. I have to do Rodney. What can I say? I adore every inch of you. But if I have to choose –

RODNEY. Don't choose.

JIMMY. But if I had to choose, I'd say your abdomen.

RODNEY. Maybe once upon a time when I had a six pack.

JIMMY. It wasn't just the six pack. It was the whole picture that was riveting.

(**JIMMY** *puts his hand under* **RODNEY**'s *shirt and caresses his stomach.* **RODNEY** *removes his hand.*)

RODNEY. That's enough.

JIMMY. Rita, your turn.

RITA. I'll start with Christina. It's your mouth.

CHRISTINA. My big fat mouth. It never shuts up.

RITA. I like the way your lips turn up at the corners even when you're unhappy.

CHRISTINA. When I was a kid, Aunt Adriana said I had blubber lips.

JIMMY. Kid, you gotta get over that. And me, Rita? What about me?

RITA. You have a very lady-like nose. A nose for trouble. I hope you pay attention to it.

JIMMY. And Rodney? Don't forget Rodney.

RITA. (*begrudgingly*) Rodney…has well groomed cuticles.

(*They all burst out laughing.* **RODNEY** *goes over to* **RITA** *and hugs her.*)

RODNEY. I think that's the most honest thing anyone has ever said to me. Thank you. A truce?

RITA. I'll think about it.

(*She sits on the far side of the sofa.*)

RODNEY. Oh come on, Rita. I'm good company in small doses. Don't sit so far away. You look like you're waiting for a bus.

CHRISTINA. Yeah, move closer.

RITA. The sofa's too crowded.

JIMMY. It makes it more cozy.

(**RITA** *joins them on the sofa, which causes* **JIMMY** *on the far arm to fall onto the floor.* **RODNEY** *is on the sofa between the two ladies.*)

CHRISTINA. Aunt Adriana, are you okay?

JIMMY. It was just a little tumble. I'm made of rubber.

RITA. But let's not forget that you've had both hips replaced.

RODNEY. My favorite place in the world is between two ladies.

JIMMY. Hey, (**JIMMY** *perches himself at the top of the sofa above* **RODNEY.**) Remember there are three of us. Rodney's angels.

(**RODNEY** *moves his face closer to* **CHRISTINA.** *She jumps up.*)

CHRISTINA. (*getting uncomfortable*) Anyone in the mood for hot cheese puffs? A Wisconsin delicacy.

JIMMY. Darling, I don't want you sequestered downstairs in that dreary kitchen. (*provocatively*) We can be perfectly satisfied with just the salami.

CHRISTINA. The cheese puffs aren't frozen. I just warm them in the toaster oven.

(*She starts to leave the room.*)

JIMMY. Don't leave.

RODNEY. I'll keep her company.

JIMMY. Don't you go too.

(**CHRISTINA** *and* **RODNEY** *exit to the stairs leading to the kitchen.*)

RITA. May I speak to you for a moment?

JIMMY. Why? All the action's in the kitchen. *(shouting)* Don't do anything without me! I'm coming!

RITA. I need to talk to you for one minute…alone.

JIMMY. What do you want?

RITA. Some answers. What the hell are you up to, dressed like that? And what happened to your wig? And going on about drag queens and Vegas impersonators. Are you nuts?

JIMMY. The most amazing thing is happening. The more I'm me, Jimmy, the better it works.

RITA. I have no idea what you're talking about.

JIMMY. It seems that the more honest you are, the more people believe you. I've been hardly making any effort at all to be Adriana. Half the time I lose the accent. I've been wearing my own clothes. Last night Christina saw me without a wig on.

RITA. What?

JIMMY. She just wants to believe. Same with the kid.

RITA. What about Rodney? He's no fool.

JIMMY. He's not as sharp as he thinks he is.

RITA. Christina's falling for him.

JIMMY. No foolin'. We've got to put the kibosh on that immediately. He'll get her all hot and bothered and before we know it, they'll be marching down the aisle to "Oh Promise Me."

RITA. She's not a dope.

JIMMY. I'm genuinely fond of that girl and I don't want her life ruined. And I want my share of the sale of this house.

RITA. He doesn't know about you, does he?

JIMMY. Of course not.

RITA. Things happen between people. You've been alone with him.

JIMMY. Nothing's happened.

RITA. You wouldn't keep that from me.

JIMMY. Why would I keep that from you? But he is wise to the fact that we want our half.

RITA. Well, what do we do about it?

JIMMY. She's just as much into you as she's into him. She's been dropping hairpins all night.

RITA. Because you've been pushing us at each other. Making her touch my face. Honestly.

JIMMY. All modesty aside, I am the puppet master. And my girl, tonight we are headed for an orgy.

RITA. I'm not getting into an orgy with you.

JIMMY. It's your opportunity to get Christina in bed.

RITA. But I want to be alone with her. I don't want to have sex with you and Rodney.

JIMMY. You won't have to. We will use Christina as bait for Rodney and Rodney as bait for Christina. But once we get them both liquored up, we separate them and lure them into our private quarters. And in doing that, we remain in a power position and can preserve our original plan.

RITA. Who do you think you're talking to? This is all just a scheme for you to have sex with Rodney. Get over it. He is one hundred per cent straight.

JIMMY. Straight into my arms, baby. Straight into my arms.

RITA. How are you going to have sex without him knowing that you're a man?

JIMMY. Tricks of the trade. Lighting. Gaffer's tape.

RITA. Jimmy, it's going to be totally one sided and it's not worth it. What's the point?

JIMMY. What's the point? To see him vulnerable. To have that one perfect moment where he's unguarded and experiencing pure rapturous pleasure...from me. But you've got to help me, Rita. You have to keep Christina away from him.

RITA. This isn't how I imagined I'd be with her. But I guess it could be fun.

JIMMY. It's gonna be great. I'll be at your side the whole time.

RITA. What?

JIMMY. Just to get things moving. Curtain's going up. Lift your breasts.

(**CHRISTINA** *and* **RODNEY** *return from the kitchen with a plate of cheese puffs.* **JIMMY** *takes* **RITA***'s hand.*)

JIMMY. *(seductively)* Hi.

Scene Four

(The living room. An hour later. **RITA** *storms down the stairs in a state of fury, followed by* **JIMMY**.*)*

RITA. I will never ever forgive you for this!

JIMMY. I could kill you!

RITA. I have so had it with you, Jimmy.

JIMMY. Don't even talk to me. You wrecked everything. You're about as sensual as a Cuisinart.

RITA. I wrecked everything? You have gotten me into some horrible, humiliating situations before but this – this –

JIMMY. Why did you have to keep criticizing him? It was like being in bed with *Rotten Tomatoes.*

RITA. Because he's a selfish pig. He just wants to be serviced.

JIMMY. I should have expected this. You were always lousy at improvisation. When we were doing the act, how many times did I have to save you?

RITA. I'm gonna spell this out so that even a sociopathic nitwit like you can understand. I am a gay woman and you made me to go down on a man. And not just any man but a man I loathe and despise.

JIMMY. No one makes anyone to do anything.

RITA. You held my head down.

JIMMY. I was guiding you. But you were so abrasive that the poor guy finally just put his panties on and fled. And took Christina with him to his room. They literally locked us out!

RITA. Can't you get it through your wig covered thick skull that the STRAIGHT PEOPLE WANTED TO HAVE SEX ALONE!

JIMMY. Well, I'm not going to give up. I'm going to get him alone. As God is my witness!

RITA. Can we talk for a minute about your priorities? You would jettison everything, all of our plans, our financial security, to have weird sex with that disgusting deadbeat.

JIMMY. I've never been in love like this before.

RITA. Love?

JIMMY. This time it's the real McCoy. I'm not brittle like you are. I've maintained a core of childlike innocence.

RITA. You need to be on meds. You really do. Lithium and salt peter.

JIMMY. Oh, what's the use of arguing? If we were younger, this would be a sexy situation. Instead, it's grotesque. Look at us.

(**CHRISTINA** *runs downstairs, followed by* **RODNEY**.)

CHRISTINA. I can't do it! I can't do it!

RODNEY. Christina! Come back! What did I do?

CHRISTINA. I can't! I can't!

JIMMY. Christina, what's going on?

(**RITA** *takes hold of* **CHRISTINA**.)

RITA. What happened? What did he do to you?

RODNEY. I didn't do anything.

CHRISTINA. It's me. It's all me.

RODNEY. All of a sudden she freaked out.

CHRISTINA. Aunt Adriana, he's yours. He's always been yours.

RODNEY. But not anymore. Not in that way.

JIMMY. Rodney, let her speak.

CHRISTINA. There we were alone in the dark. And you were on top of me. And all I could see was Aunt Adriana's face. I knew that I was betraying her.

RODNEY. But we're not together any more.

CHRISTINA. Any fool can see that you're still in love. You have a chemistry that's undeniable. I flashbacked to my parents and how they were passionately attracted to each other till the day my father died. I was in the way then. I won't be in the way now.

RODNEY. But we've always had an open relationship. From the very beginning. Adriana is European. Group sex. Voyeurism. We've done it all.

JIMMY. I feel differently now.

CHRISTINA. You and Aunt Adriana were meant to be together. Rita, I'm right. Aren't I?

RITA. They're two of a kind.

CHRISTINA. Aunt Adriana, I don't want to be your competition. I want to be family. I made up my mind last night while I was washing out your wig. I'm going to split the money with you.

RITA. Blessed Mother of God.

CHRISTINA. Rita, you really think you can sell this house for twelve million dollars?

RITA. The house on the corner went for nearly twenty.

CHRISTINA. Well, Rachel and I can certainly get by on half of that. Aunt Adriana, I haven't known you very long. I don't count anything prior to this visit, but last night we really stripped down to our essence. There was no play acting involved. I loved the person I was with last night. And I want you to be financially at ease, so it's all settled.

*(***CHRISTINA*** joins ***JIMMY*** on the sofa and embraces him.)*

RODNEY. Well, this is fantastic! Wonderful news! Christina, you're a good girl.

*(He gives ***CHRISTINA*** a big hug.)*

CHRISTINA. Ow. You're hurting me.

*(***RACHEL*** comes downstairs holding a brown paper bag.)*

CHRISTINA. Oh honey, did we wake you up?

RACHEL. There was no way I was going to sleep tonight.

CHRISTINA. Oliver knew that I was going to break the news to you some time soon. *(to ***RACHEL***)* I just told them.

RODNEY. What's in that bag?

RACHEL. Nothing much. Just evidence of your crimes.

CHRISTINA. Baby, what are you saying?

(She has in one hand a small tack.)

RACHEL. Mother, does this look familiar?

CHRISTINA. I don't have my glasses on.

RACHEL. It's a tack. Is it the same kind that was in your vitamins?

(CHRISTINA *moves closer and examines it.*)

CHRISTINA. It *is* the same kind.

RACHEL. I found a bag of them in Rodney's room. Yes, Rodney, while you were out today, I ransacked your room. I went through all your precious things.

RODNEY. It's going to take a lot for me to forgive you.

RITA. This is outrageous. Christina, did you swallow a tack?

CHRISTINA. I caught it just in time. I thought it was an accident.

RITA. Just like the cellar step being broken?

RACHEL. You've been trying to kill my mother, you sick fuck.

RODNEY. Hey, you're too young to call me that. Yes, I bought the tacks. I was going to surprise Adriana by fixing that broken chair.

RITA. Come on. You can do better than that.

RODNEY. A lot of things are broken in this house, including the cellar steps.

CHRISTINA. You tried to kill me! Twice!

RACHEL. You mother fucking pig bastard psychopath!

RODNEY. I'm an easy target.

RITA. Because you're guilty!

RODNEY. Accuse the guy who's down and out.

RACHEL. Explain away this!

(RACHEL *removes a smaller bag within the bag.*)

CHRISTINA. That was in the refrigerator.

RODNEY. Hand it right over. I'm not kidding around.

RACHEL. Aunt Adriana told me that you were in the body organ trafficking market in Romania.

RODNEY. *(to* JIMMY*)* You told her?

JIMMY. I thought it made you look better.

RACHEL. What I have here is a fresh batch of human fingernails.

JIMMY. You're still at it?

RODNEY. I sell them under the table to a company that does cosmetic testing. I'm a go-between.

RACHEL. Those other bags in the refrigerator contain spines, ears and some strange things that look like frozen chicken cutlets.

RODNEY. They're all necessary for scientific research.

RACHEL. And guess what's in the fur vault in the cellar. The corpse of an old woman.

CHRISTINA. *(This is just toooo much.)* Oh no. That's just not right.

RODNEY. It'll be gone by tomorrow morning. There was a shipping problem.

RITA. A shipping problem? Where? From Amazon?

RODNEY. Okay, look. I'm in over my head in something revolting and illegal. But I'm not the only one here acting out of desperation.

RACHEL. *You're* guilty of attempted murder, you twisted ass wipe.

CHRISTINA. Yeah. When you were planning on finishing *that* job?

RODNEY. It was nothing personal. You were in the way.

CHRISTINA. The story of my life!

RACHEL. How could you profit from Mom's death? Were you hoping that Aunt Adriana would give you some of the money from the sale of the house?

RITA. Don't you think she'd suspect that a third accident might have been foul play?

CHRISTINA. What could you possibly have on Aunt Adriana that would make her agree to be an accessory to a murder?

RODNEY. *(to* **JIMMY***)* Would you care to answer their questions?

JIMMY. Mmmmm. I'd rather not.

RODNEY. Allow me to introduce you to Jimmy Nichols.

CHRISTINA. Jimmy?

RITA. He knows! He does know!!

RODNEY. I know that Jimmy is a professional female impersonator. I know he rented a room from Adriana and was present when she died of natural causes. We'll grant him that. And with the aid of our sanctimonious pal, Rita, he sent Adriana's body off to the coroner with a fake ID. With him posing as Adriana, they attempted to sell this house and cheat you out of your inheritance.

JIMMY. Adriana led us to believe she had no heirs.

RACHEL. So you're not transsexual?

JIMMY. No.

CHRISTINA. You're a drag queen and have been posing as Aunt Adriana all this time?

JIMMY. I'm not a drag queen. I'm a tribute artist. But yes, I was posing as your Aunt.

RITA. You told me to my face that Rodney didn't know about you.

JIMMY. *(lying across the sofa)* What can I say? I'm a liar. I've always been a liar. I'm so tired, so tired of lying and making up lies. Not knowing what is a lie and what's the truth.

RITA. He's doing Mary Astor in *The Maltese Falcon*. Why didn't you tell me Rodney was blackmailing you?

JIMMY. He said if I told you the truth, he would kill you.

RODNEY. I didn't say that.

JIMMY. You implied it, you sick fuck.

RODNEY. *(with vulnerable intimacy)* Jimmy, listen to me. You probably know me better than anyone I've ever met. You've taken the time to push and prod me into being my authentic self. Tell them who I really am and what made me this way.

RACHEL. Don't you dare try to con him, you worthless piece of shit.

CHRISTINA. Rachel! Oliver!

JIMMY. Let me tell you something. You're a fake. And you'll end your life in the gutter, because the gutter's where you came from and the gutter's where you belong.

RITA. Rosalind Russell. *Picnic.*

JIMMY. Christina, when we started this scheme, I never thought of you as a real person. You were just someone in the way. I'm so sorry. It's your money. Your house. Take all of it.

RODNEY. Easy to say now that you're exposed.

CHRISTINA. I should be furious, but somehow I feel incredibly relieved that you're not really Adriana. She was so cruel to me when I was a child. I've spent thirty years hating her.

RACHEL. Mom, you wanted a mother but you got a funny gay brother.

(JIMMY *bursts into tears.*)

CHRISTINA. You're crying.

RITA. Are you really crying? You're not doing Meryl Streep or Margaret O'Brien, are you?

JIMMY. No. No movie.

RODNEY. This mockery of sentimentality is making me gag.

JIMMY. I'm glad you understand the strength of sentiment, because its beauty is something you will never know.

RITA. Norma Shearer in *The Women.*

JIMMY. Would you please stop annotating me?

RITA. The majority of the people in this room don't know your references!!

RACHEL. Rodney, you're going down. I'm calling the police.

RODNEY. Then would you please put me on the line? I'd like to tell them that your Mom's living on stolen credit cards. Yeah. I'd say I'm calling the shots in this game.

CHRISTINA. *(with a wonderful new strength)* Oh, I knew there was something I meant to tell you. This morning I phoned my friend Melanie's husband and confessed that I stole her credit cards. I forgot what a great guy he is. He totally understood that I was having a breakdown. And I promised that as soon as I get my inheritance I would not only pay him back but make a sizeable donation to the foundation he's creating in Melanie's name. So, Rodney, if you think for even a second about causing trouble for anyone in this room, I'll turn you in and you'll be doing at least twenty years in the slammer.

RODNEY. I'll be gone before any of you get up. Where I'll go, what will happen to me, I don't know. Not that any one of you give a damn about my situation, but here I am raised by a bi-polar heroin addict, emotionally and sexually abused since I can remember, caught in the web of a predatory older woman and being so crushed by her merciless narcissism that I wound up a drug addict on skid row, only to be years later, jerked out of a hard won sobriety by an emotionally disturbed gender bending teenager, with the promise of a kind of spiritual salvation but find myself instead sexually harassed and pursued by a grifter drag queen and a mid-western credit card scam artist, who I did my best to encourage and build sexual confidence in herself, and in return, haven't received an ounce of sympathy or understanding that perhaps I had valid personal reasons for "creating accidents" that might *possibly* have harmed her but didn't, and anyway should be proof positive that rather than being a victim of misfortune, she actually lives under a lucky star to have escaped injury so often, but of course, no thanks come my way and indeed to top it off, I'm stripped naked and forced against my will to endure an excruciatingly painful blow job from a man hating lesbian. Well, as they say, life isn't fair. I'm going. I can't go soon enough. I have witnessed unspeakable horrors in all four corners of the world; slavery, torture, cannibalism, but I have never encountered a more vile, hypocritical, insincere, morally corrupt group than those living under this hateful roof and if there's any justice, I hope it caves in on all of you. I'll have someone pick up the body tomorrow. Good night.

(He exits the house.)

JIMMY. So, kids, where do we go from here?

RITA. The immediate plan is we put the house back on the market first thing in the morning.

RACHEL. Mom, we're going to stay in New York, aren't we?

CHRISTINA. Oliver, this city is our haven. We've been here over a month. We're New Yorkers!

RITA. Christina, I have on my books a great two bedroom in Chelsea. Twenty-four hour doorman. Fitness Center. No board approval. Jimmy, you and I can now both afford luxury one bedrooms. Mine will be on the Upper West Side and yours very far downtown. It's a real estate bonanza.

RACHEL. Jimmy, you can't go on being Aunt Adriana. We have to report her death. That must have been part of your original plan.

JIMMY. After we sold the house, we were going to go to Europe and say she died there.

RACHEL. But don't you need a body to report a death?

JIMMY. You don't think they would just take our word? I mean, it's Europe.

CHRISTINA. You really aren't detail people. What are we going to do? We need to produce a body.

RITA. There's always a fly in the ointment.

JIMMY. The solution is right underneath us. The fur fault. The last I heard there was a woman in mothballs hanging between the coats.

CHRISTINA. But she belongs to Rodney.

RITA. Well, he's not getting her back! She's gonna have to be Adriana.

RACHEL. *(gleefully)* He'll be so pissed!

JIMMY. We'll get the police to remove the body first thing tomorrow morning before Rodney can make any other plans. Can we just say it? This is genius. It's fool proof!

CHRISTINA. Oliver, it's going to be a new life for us. We're going to educate ourselves. We're going to go to the theatre and the opera and the ballet. Do you know what I did this afternoon? I bought you a tuxedo. It's the neatest thing.

RACHEL. A tuxedo? With the vest and bow tie and everything? Was it very expensive?

CHRISTINA. Who cares? We're rich. It's in my room. Wanna see it?

RACHEL. Wanna see it? I want to try it on right now!

CHRISTINA. *(overjoyed to the point of tears)* He likes something I bought him!!

*(They run upstairs. **JIMMY** collapses into a chair.)*

JIMMY. Ohhhhh, this was a tough one. But I suppose in some ways it was worth it just for the sake of the anecdotes. But why do you want to live so far apart? Wouldn't it be fun to be neighbors in the same building, Ethel?

RITA. I don't want to see that much of you.

JIMMY. I'm too tired to joke.

RITA. You're not good for me.

JIMMY. Rita–.

RITA. You betrayed me. You lied to my face. You chose sex over a twenty year friendship. I can never trust you again.

JIMMY. This was an extraordinary situation.

RITA. It revealed our true characters. I see now that I've always been more of a friend to you than you've been to me. So if that's the case, I have to protect myself and not look to you for more than what you can offer. I'll be your real estate agent and in the morning we'll deal with the lady in the fur vault. But after that you're on your own.

(**RITA** *turns to go up the stairs, then stops and turns around.*)

RITA. Well, how was that for improvisational skills?

JIMMY. What? Everything you said–?

RITA. Did you really think I was serious?

JIMMY. Yes! You were brilliant!

RITA. *(pouring them both glasses of wine)* So how's this? There are two one bedrooms available in that fabulous building at the corner of Twelfth Street. Parquet floors, sub-zero refrigerator, Viking stove, health club with lap pool.

JIMMY. I love that building. It's so grand. I hope I can walk through that lobby and not feel totally intimidated. I may have to use a British accent.

RITA. Just be yourself and ring for the elevator.

JIMMY. I totally forgot. I had a mad, passionate affair with a wealthy sculptor who lived in that building. His stuff went for thousands. And I think his family owned like all the artichokes in the United States.

RITA. I remember him. He looked like an artichoke.

JIMMY. No. He was very sexy. I was way too immature and he was so much older than me. Mmmmm. I wonder if he still lives there.

RITA. Do the math. He'd be a hundred and two years old.

JIMMY. A hundred and two is the new ninety. And well, six million dollars doesn't get you very far these days.

RITA. So what's your angle?

JIMMY. No angle. Just matrimony.

RITA. Jimmy –

JIMMY. I mean, you never know…

JIMMY/RITA. Said the widow.

(*The two old friends clink glasses and continue to laughingly conspire.*)

End of Play

9 780573 702860